UNCONTACTED

RICK CHESLER

CHAPTER 1

Brazilian Amazon, near the Peruvidan border

The Huntair Pathfinder Mark 1 ultralight aircraft banked over a group of treetops that themselves towered above the rest of the rain forest canopy. The single-occupant plane carried a man who had devoted his entire professional career to studying the world's rain forests, and the Amazon in particular. Dr. Antonio Medina, a professor of ecology and a researcher working out of a major Texas university, had outfitted his little craft with state-of-the-art scientific equipment to within an inch of its already low weight capacity.

He checked his array of sensors, grinning at the row of green lights indicating everything was A-OK. Antonio was extremely proud of his "air-based sensory observation platform (ABSOP)," which had cost him countless late nights applying for grants and seeking corporate backing to fund. But here he was, counting the trees and gauging the thickness of individual branches, collecting all manner of environmental data including temperature, wind speed, humidity, barometer, albedo, as well as taking high resolution photographs and video of everything he flew over.

He brought his plane in low over a sun-dappled river, its brown surface meandering through the green like a snake through a field. He grinned ear to ear as he followed the waterway's course, threading the needle between the banks of thick trees on either side. He'd used the Huntair for many research trips before this one, but the thrill never got old. He had trained a couple of other members of his expedition team to be able to fly it, just in case the need arose, but it rarely did. This was one job Antonio was more than happy to handle on his own.

He heard a squawk and turned his head left in time to see a black-collared hawk come very close to his aircraft before veering away and dropping low out of sight. But it wasn't only the joy of flying, the sense of freedom it provided, he knew. It was deeper than that. It made him feel closer to his father, Diego Medina, who had been born in Brazil before moving to the United States as a boy and becoming a citizen there.

Like Antonio, Diego had been a rain forest researcher. Also like Antonio, he had pioneered the use of ultralight aircraft as a research tool to study the jungle. In his day, the craft were even more precarious than they were now, and it simply wasn't possible to carry the bulky scientific instruments of that time. Nevertheless, by utilizing the frail contraptions to conduct aerial surveys from areas that were inaccessible by any other means—including helicopter—he had demonstrated unequivocally that the ultralight had a rightful place in cutting edge rain forest research. And in the process, he had shown his son that studying the rain forest could be very "cool" indeed.

His father had flown his Pterodactyl Ascender over these same Amazonian jungles, exploring the mysteries of the rain forest until one day...the crash. Twenty years ago. Antonio remembered the fateful trip well, because he was on it. To then twenty-six year old Antonio, having earned his own PhD only a few months earlier, the opportunity to work with his father had seemed like a dream come true.

The winds had been a little higher than normal that day and the members of the expedition team had urged him not to go up. Regretfully, Antonio recalled, he had not cautioned him to stay on the ground. It was his first research trip with his father, who had set the expedition up –his first professional expedition at all, for that matter—so who was he to tell him what to do? So he had said nothing, and even though the other team members had cautioned against it, his father had gone aloft, pointing out they had only one more field day before needing to begin the multi-stage return trip home.

Diego Medina's ultralight would be discovered wrapped around one of the canopy trees, about halfway up. Hopelessly mangled, and a total loss. The wreck didn't seem survivable for any mortal man, that was for sure. The impact alone should have killed any passenger who wasn't superhuman. And then there was the sobering thought that, even if he had survived the impact, that the fall to the ground almost certainly would have been fatal.

But his body wasn't in the wreckage and it wasn't on the ground at the base of the tree. Or anywhere nearby. The expedition had mounted a thorough search on their own for the next twenty-four straight hours, but no sign of him turned up. After that, Brazilian authorities had mounted their own recovery mission, but they, too, had come up empty. Perhaps his body was carried away by predators, they had offered. Or, they had added in response to the doubting looks, maybe he fell out of the plane *before* it crashed, and that's why it lost control. Heavy turbulence, wind pockets, or simply reckless flying? It was a windy day, they had noted. Was he in the habit of wearing the seatbelt? (Yes). Did he drink? (Sometimes, but he was never under the influence while flying). All these questions and more were bandied about, but none of them changed the end result. Twenty years on, Dr. Diego Medina's body was still missing.

Antonio could still recall the last words his father had ever said to him: "There's still more data to collect—a lot more!" They haunted him to this day. He was right, of course. But that wasn't it. The lack of closure was no doubt one factor that kept him returning to the Amazon all these years—decades—later. It made him feel closer to his father, and what's more, there was always that hope against hope that he would hear something from a villager or expeditioner. But no word ever came.

But he had to work, too, like anyone else, and so that also kept him coming back. Still, he knew that the entire Amazon was much larger than the sector in which his father had disappeared. If he was to view a plot of his research study areas on a map, they would be mostly concentrated in the area near where his father went missing. On this trip, though, he'd ventured farther afield, so that was something. Branching out, moving on, learning, expanding…

Antonio pulled up on the stick of the craft and rose above the wall of trees that was rapidly approaching, rather than follow the river's tightly winding course down low. His own research was going fairly well, he thought, once again eyeing his extensive (and expensive) on-board instrumentation. He was slowly but surely putting together the most comprehensive, data-rich map of the Amazon ever produced. And then would come the real work, he knew--analyzing the data, studying how it all fit together, and explaining what made this unique environment tick.

His thoughts were interrupted by the bleating of his air band radio. The voice was in Portuguese, a language he was familiar with but not fluent in. He had always told his father, who had been fluent, being born in Brazil, that he wished he would have taught it to him. But Diego had blamed it on his mother's early death from cancer, on how being a widower and single Dad uncomfortable with the dating scene while trying to move forward with his career had left him with little time. Still, Antonio caught the gist of the words, "have urgent communication for you from the Office of the President of Brazil," and raised an eyebrow.

Probably just want to hassle me about inspecting my permits again. He had a pretty good working relationship with the government of Brazil—he had to in order to conduct his research here—but like any bureaucratic system, there was no small amount of red tape to deal with. And because he used an airplane, that just added to the rigmarole. He sighed and glanced at his fuel gauge. Time to head back to base camp, refuel and get some lunch, then head back out for a late afternoon pass.

He consulted his GPS unit and made a minor adjustment to his ultralight's heading. Even to an experienced Amazon traveler, the forest looked much the same in every direction from the air. His landing strip (and

4

even that phrase implied more grandiosity than the bare minimum clearing that had been hastily hacked out of the jungle by his team) wasn't far away. As he always did, Antonio blocked out all other thoughts as he prepared for the landing. All it took was one tricky updraft as he passed over the tree line into the clearing, one lapse of attention, to catch a wingtip on the canopy and go cartwheeling into oblivion…as perhaps his father had done those decades ago?

Antonio shoved the uncomfortable thought aside and gripped the stick. He spoke into his radio transmitter to inform his team he was coming in for a landing so that they could make sure it was clear, and be standing by to render assistance should his landing be less than perfect. He heard the *copy that* response and then committed fully to bringing the ultralight down.

Thankfully, no surprises awaited him and the touchdown was as smooth as could be. A couple of bounces on the landing gear and he was rolling across the cut clearing, no sticks larger than a twig in his way on the ground. He braked to a stop mere yards before the strip emptied out into the river, but that was nothing new. It was a lot of work to clear the jungle, so they gave him what the plane's specs said it needed, and not much more. Antonio killed the engine and hopped down from his cockpit while three members of his dozen-person team ran up to greet him.

Two of them were graduate student research assistants whom he had specially trained on flight operations, so he wasn't surprised to see them. They would take over the plane's handling on the ground, wheel it over to the makeshift fuel station and get it ready for the next flight. But he was a little taken aback to see his colleague, Dr. Peter Richards. Richards was a U.S. researcher from a different university, but a close collaborator and co-author on many of his research papers. He would have thought he'd be hunched over a laptop in the lab tent, examining the ultralight's telemetry data as it streamed in.

Richards towered over Antonio's own nearly six-foot frame, his bald dome in contrast to Antonio's thick head of black curly hair. He was out of breath from running out to greet him. He spoke breathlessly to Antonio while the assistants fussed over the ultralight and its post-flight checklist.

"Antonio, the Brazilian government says they've been trying to reach you via air band, did you—"

"I heard them, I figured it could wait 'til I got back on the ground. I mean geez, the paperwork is all in order, we triple-checked it before we left, what do they—"

But Richards shook his head emphatically. "No, Antonio, it's not routine. Some kind of situation has come up and they're requesting your assistance."

Antonio frowned. "Did you offer to help?"

"Of course, but they said they need aerial assistance. They wanted to talk to you personally, since you're the one with the actual flight permit."

Antonio nodded and waved toward the jungle camp. "Let's go have a chat with them."

They walked away from the gurgling, brown river onto a barely discernable footpath that led them through a thick stand of thorny foliage a short distance until it opened into a natural clearing where a multitude of tents had been erected. Other members of the team bustled about here, one working on getting a cook fire going, another sitting at a folding table and working with some camera equipment, while others could be heard conversing in the larger work tents.

It was into one of these that Antonio and Richards walked, the one that served as their Communications Tent. In it they had a series of folding tables supporting rows of laptop computers, radio equipment and satellite telephones. A thirty-ish American man with long, dirty-blond hair tied back in a ponytail waved them over without looking up from his workstation.

"Office of the Brazilian President on a VHF channel. His people are annoyed you haven't responded yet." He got up from the chair and indicated for Antonio to have a seat in front of the radio's microphone. Antonio thanked the technician and spoke into the mic.

"Dr. Antonio Medina, speaking." He released the transmitter button and waited for the reply, which was not long in coming.

"Dr. Medina, this is Olivia Clara, from the Brazil Office of Cultural Affairs," the female voice over the radio came back in accented English.

"Do you make it a habit of not responding to urgent air band requests?"

Antonio looked at Richards, who grimaced before motioning to the mic. Antonio replied into it. "I apologize, Senhora Clara. I did hear part of the request, but at the time I was—"

"Never mind that now, Doctor. We have an urgent request, and I am going to put President Rocha on now to convey it."

Antonio and Richards exchanged puzzled glances. The president of Brazil wanted to talk to Antonio? Certainly this was no permitting snafu or work visa inquiry. He responded over the radio.

"Of course, standing by."

A few seconds passed during which light static was heard, and then an elderly male voice, also in accented English, emanated from the tinny speaker. "Dr. Medina, thank you for taking the time to speak with me. We haven't yet had the pleasure of meeting in person, although our Ministry of Scientific Research has made me aware of your activities—in a most positive way, I can assure you. Let me add that I am also aware of the high quality research your father conducted in our country, and I do of course offer my condolences on his accident, even though much time has passed. Forgive me, senhor, but time constraints demand that I move our conversation along. I trust your research is going well?"

Richards winked at Antonio and gave him the thumbs up sign. *So far so good.* At least it didn't seem like they were about to be personally ordered to leave the country by the president himself. The technician stood at the entrance to the tent, as if standing watch, expecting a national guard platoon to come rolling up at any moment.

Antonio continued with the radio. "Very well, Mr. President, thank you for asking, and thank you for your condolences. To what do I owe the pleasure of your radio call to our humble jungle camp?"

Richards nodded. *Get right to the point.* The president answered.

"A situation has developed that you may be able to assist us with. I understand it would take up your valuable research time, but in return I am of course prepared to extend your visa for as long as necessary, as well as providing reasonable, though not extravagant, financial compensation."

"My team and I are happy to assist your government, senhor. Please let me know what you need."

"Thank you, Dr. Medina. There has been an unfortunate event that is soon to hit the news wires. Even from your humble jungle camp, as you call it, I am certain that you will hear of it over the radio. So let me give you the news first." The president paused.

"Listening, Mr. President."

Brazil's leader continued to transmit. "Less than an hour ago, hundreds of people were killed in several of my country's jungle cities, as well as at least one in Peru: Iquitos, Santarém, Belém, Manaus, and Macapá. At latest count, the death toll stood at 484 people all told; men, women and children."

Shocked silence reigned for a moment until the president asked if the connection was still good.

"Yes, we are here," Antonio transmitted. "Just stunned, trying to process the terrible news. What happened to these people? Has there been a terrorist attack?" At the door, the technician glanced up to the sky, as if expecting an air raid of some sort at any second.

The president's voice came back over the speaker. "We are not yet certain, but if it is, it is the strangest terror attack the world has ever seen." He paused without elaborating, so Antonio voiced the question on his and Richards' minds.

"How did these people die?"

The president cleared his throat before answering. "We're still not exactly sure—autopsies are being conducted as we speak—but it appears as though they all literally dropped dead of natural causes. Their hearts simply stopped beating, their brain activity ceased, and they died. One observer in Manaus said it was as if the people simply 'expired' without warning."

Antonio and Richards traded looks, during which Richards mouthed the word, *poison?*

"Do you suspect a terror attack by poison, Mr. President?" Antonio was beginning to wonder why the president wanted to speak with him about this matter that seemed more suited for the military.

"We have no reason to think as such at this time."

"Perhaps the water supply has been poisoned in the Amazon basin?" Antonio threw out.

"We considered that possibility, but it doesn't explain why only some people died. Many more thousands of persons living in those cities drank the water than the 500 or so who died, and no one else is even sick."

Puzzled silence once again filled the tent and the airwaves. "It must be some sort of targeted attack, sir," Antonio began. "What else could—" But the president cut him off.

"Targeted, perhaps, yes. But it still doesn't seem like terrorism. Let me explain. There is something I have not yet told you. Something I would like to remain confidential for as long as possible, though it is doubtful that will last long."

"The information will not leave our camp unless directed by your office, sir."

"Thank you. First of all, every one of the victims was a tribal descendant of indigenous rain forest peoples found in either the Brazilian or Peruvian Amazon."

"Sounds like maybe a hate crime, then?"

"Perhaps. But there is one more thing. Something quite odd. All of the victims share the same birthday."

"Exactly the same?"

"Not the same year—the deceased are of many ages, young and old— but every single one of them, so far as we can tell through identification and reports from next of kin, was born on the same day: February 29."

CHAPTER 2

Antonio swatted a weird-looking bug off his shoulder while he tried to process what he was hearing in the communications tent. "February 29th, that's leap day."

The radio crackled with the Brazilian president's response. "Correct. Very strange. My people are looking into it now, whether this can be some sort of hoax. But listen, as I said, time is short, and there is something I need you to do for me."

"Go ahead with the details, Mr. President." Antonio and Richards leaned in closer to the radio's speaker.

"I would like for you to visit some of the tribes in your area and see if they are okay. Pay a visit to them and just check up on them and see if anything seems unusual. Do they have any deaths? Illnesses? If your communication skills are sufficient, you may tell them I asked you to check up on them in light of recent events, otherwise, simply visit them and report back on what you find. Can you do that?"

Antonio and Richards nodded to one another. It was something they could do easily enough. They had come into contact with some of the tribal people of the Amazon now and then over the years. Antonio pressed the transmitter.

"Affirmative, Mr. President. We'll get going right away and report back by end of day."

The president breathed an audible sigh of relief over the radio. "Thank you so much. You have no idea how much this means to me. We have people en route as well, but as you know the jungle is vast, and you are already in the middle of it."

Antonio signed off and turned to Richards. "What do you say we split our team up into two groups of five: so we have two left over to stay here to mind the camp, and five each head out in different directions to make tribal contact."

"I head up one contact team and you head up the other?"

Antonio nodded. He and Richards, both in their late forties, were by far the most experienced members of the outfit, so the choice made sense. "Let's get set up to move out."

#

Three hours later, Antonio and his team of four other expedition members—three graduate students and a professional lab technician--made the first tribal contact. After the sweat-drenched, bug-infested hike through jungle that needed to be constantly kept at bay with machetes, it was a relief to hear the voices of other humans, indicating that their long trek was coming to an end.

For Antonio in particular, he was reassured, since he hadn't been positive they'd come across a tribe here. The indigenous people didn't always stay in the same location for very long. What's more, Antonio himself was not an expert on tribal people—he was an ecologist, not an anthropologist—but fortunately his ultralight work had enabled him to see the locations of tribes in the area in recent years, and this one, at least, was still in the same place.

His team, with him in the lead, trooped in single file along a narrow game path until they reached a tree with a multitude of arrows stuck into it. A warning. A signpost. *You have arrived at our place.* No sooner had Antonio acknowledged the arrows than a tribal man, slight of stature but lithe, wiry and sinewy, stepped from the riotous plant life without a sound.

He carried a short wooden spear but smiled upon seeing the newcomers. He said a couple of words in his native language that Antonio recognized from previous encounters as a friendly greeting. Antonio held a hand back to his team, telling them to wait in place. Then he repeated one of the same words back to the tribal man, whom Antonio knew was a lookout for his people, responsible for alerting them to approaching danger.

Antonio pointed to himself and then his group, and then gestured to the tribal man and beyond him, where his camp was. He could hear activity there, the normal hubbub of daily tribal routine, water being splashed as cookware was washed, children laughing, roosters crowing and dogs barking.

"You go?" the guard said in the broken Portuguese that was his only connection to modern day language. Antonio and the rest of them nodded enthusiastically, and the tribal man beckoned to them as he turned and jogged down the path.

After a short distance they reached a large circular clearing with a few wooden longhouses along the far edge. Clusters of tribal people were gathered here and there—a group of women around a cookpot, some men untangling a large fishing net, a group of children kicking a soccer ball around. It was plain to see that these people had plenty of contact with the modern world: several of them wore T-shirts with corporate logos on them, a few wore shoes, a couple that Antonio saw even wore digital wristwatches. He knew from experience that they liked them because they were shiny baubles, but they could care less about using them to tell time. They knew what time it was by the position of the sun in the sky. They went to sleep and woke up each morning with the kind of regularity one gets when one doesn't sleep longer on the weekends because she has to get up early the other five days of the week, Antonio mused.

All told, he thought, gazing around the settlement, it looked pretty much like business as usual for an Amazonian tribe. No one seemed upset, and he certainly couldn't see any evidence of recent deaths or mourning. But he had come all this way specifically to make sure, so some level of communication would be required.

While his team traded items with the tribe members (candy bars were always popular, as were simple manufactured items like pens, lighters, pen knives, etc.), Antonio pointed to the central longhouse and pantomimed himself going inside it to a group of men who had walked over to greet him. Most wore loincloths only and were extensively tattooed, but a few of them wore at least one western clothing item. Once they figured out he was asking permission to enter the structure, they nodded enthusiastically and ushered him right to the steps of the open-air building. It had partial walls built of thatched palm, and a roof, but there was a gap from ceiling to the top of the wall, to facilitate air circulation.

Antonio entered, accompanied by one of the tribesmen, who chattered excitedly in his native language to the other people inside, a group of elder men and women, smoking a pungent-smelling herb that Antonio recognized as rapé. Antonio was not an expert on tribal structure, but he knew enough to realize that these were the elder statesmen of the group, the leaders. Knowing his tribal dialect would be woefully insufficient to get his point across, he tried his best Portuguese on them, explaining that he wanted to know if everyone in the tribe was okay, if anything bad or strange had happened lately.

The elders bore confused looks on their faces as they turned heads, looking at each other, bewildered. They all shook their heads at him. Enough Portuguese was spoken for Antonio to get that no one they knew had died recently, except for a wild boar they had kept as a pet for many years. Antonio thanked them, left an offering of assorted modern day items that were fascinating and useful to the tribe and their children—combs, fidget spinners, fishing line, chewing gum, squirt guns, lighters--and then exited the longhouse.

Back in the outdoor common area, Antonio met up with his team members and asked them if they had turned anything up. None of them reported anything other than typical trading interactions, and so they bid the tribe goodbye and set off back through the jungle to their camp.

#

Back at camp, Antonio found Richards' team already there, having returned from their own excursion. He caught up with Richards in the kitchen tent, where he was helping prepare the night's meal of fresh caught river fish, canned beans, and s'mores for dessert.

"How'd it go?" Antonio picked up a can opener and began helping his friend prepare the food.

Richards shrugged and shook his head. "We located the Caimbé tribe, but they said they were fine, and everything seemed totally normal. No one dying or anything like that we could tell."

Antonio related his own team's similar experience. "What do you say tomorrow we try the same thing one more time?"

Richards agreed. "I think the gang's up for it."

Antonio dried his hands on a dish cloth. "I'll head over to the comm tent and update President Rocha on our progress."

#

Almost twenty-four hours later, the full team was assembled back in the jungle camp after another outing seeking contact with tribes even further afield than the ones of the previous day. Like yesterday, both sub-teams had again made contact with a tribe, but also like yesterday, neither tribe reported anything out of the ordinary, nor had they even heard of anything unusual. It seemed to be just another day of life in the Amazon.

As they sat around a fire eating dinner, all of them remarked how tired and sore they were from the long hikes. Their usual research didn't normally require such arduous treks. While the grad students and techs compared war wounds—blisters, scratches, insect bites, minor bruises—Richards asked Antonio if he'd contacted the president yet.

"Soon as the meal's done." He washed down a bite of fish with a can of Guarana soda. "Wanted to solidify our plans first, before I talk to him."

Richards shot him a concerned glance. "Our plans are to get back to our research, right? I mean, we do have our own work to do..."

"Right, but I was thinking there's one more thing we can try to help with this situation."

"I'm all ears."

"In the morning, I'd like to take the ultralight up and have a look to the northeast, see if I can reach one of the tribes out that way. Different direction than we've hit so far."

Richards let his fork fall onto his plate. "Antonio, there are no settlements in that direction for...I don't know how far."

Antonio nodded rapidly. "That's the whole point. Things might be different out that way. I just figure, since we have the plane, that it might be worth a look."

"What are the chances you'll be able to land, even if you do see a tribe out there? I doubt they'll be so accommodating as to clear you a landing strip on sight. And they don't use radios."

Antonio shot him a mock smile. "Really? Gee, I guess you're right. But still, simply by flying in low, I might be able to see if anything seems out of whack. Then I'll mark the position and return to camp. After that, we would have the option of going to it on foot, after talking to the president to confirm that's what he wants."

Richards stroked the stubble on his chin while shaking his head slowly. "Hey, I know it can't hurt for us to get in the president's good graces, but even if they pay for everything and support us..." He glanced at his digital watch. "...we've all got other obligations to get back to at home, Antonio. This grant is not the only thing on my plate right now, you know that."

"Of course. Look, how about this: we spend one more day on this— tomorrow—that's it. I'll fly up, take a look, and then I'll radio Brazil the coordinates of any settlements I come across if they're more than a day away for us. That way they know we've done our part, even gone above and beyond a little bit. Without their support, Peter, this research wouldn't even be possible. We depend on working down here for a lot of our grants, not only this one. And, keep in mind: I can still run the science platform to collect more data while I'm flying, so we'll still be furthering our research agenda."

At length, Richards nodded. "Fair enough. But you better be airborne at first light."

#

The next morning, Antonio watched the sunrise break over the canopy from the cockpit of his Huntair Pathfinder. Even this early, and a hundred feet off the ground, the air was warm and sticky. He'd taken a small backpack with him, knowing he'd need items to trade if he did encounter a tribe, and that meant he had to hunch forward in his seat, but so far he was okay with that. One thing he noticed right away, though, was a lack of air currents. There was almost no wind, which made for smooth flying that would allow for maximum range. He knew the winds tended to pick up a bit in the afternoon, but hopefully he could make a contact and be back at camp by then.

A flock of birds took wing from the canopy beneath him as he checked his compass heading and adjusted his course toward the vast, unbroken expanse of greenery that lay toward Peru. So primal, he thought, gazing down at the primary growth rain forest. For all the reports of logging and clearing for palm oil plantations—and those were serious ecological threats—the Amazon still reigned supreme as one of the last unbroken wildernesses on the planet. Endless hectares of trees—an ocean of chlorophyll—spread out beneath him as he coasted over in his fragile craft.

Antonio was under no illusion that spotting a tribal settlement, even from his bird-like perch, would be a simple matter. He had to keep his eyes constantly trained far enough ahead that he could look for breaks in the canopy—areas where a tribe would have a settlement—and then peer straight down as he passed directly overhead. And all that while maintaining his awareness of the plane's instrumentation. Even though this was a flight with a different purpose, as he had promised Richards, he also kept the research gadgets in operation—the science platform of sensors and gauges.

He kept his focus in this manner as early morning transitioned into mid-

and then late morning. He made hourly radio contact with his camp as he continued to fly deeper into the rain forest. So far there was nothing noteworthy to report. After a while the monotonous drone of his ultralight's whiny engine, along with the never-ending carpet of green below, combined to cause him to almost nod off. When he jerked awake after hearing a thin canopy-top branch whip the undercarriage of his plane, Antonio knew he had to snap out of it. He reached into a pocket of his pants and removed a small canteen that he'd filled with coffee from this morning's camp breakfast. Cold by now, but who cares? He took his hands off the plane's controls just long enough to unscrew the lid and then chugged back the caffeinated liquid.

As he flew on, he became aware that the topography of the jungle was changing. No longer an uninterrupted flat basin, he began to see hilltops rising and falling—green humps covered with trees. He checked his fuel gauge, knowing this meant he had ventured far from his camp. He was okay for now. And then he saw it. Ahead, rising from the jungle floor was a large, verdant hill, or maybe even a small mountain.

Antonio aimed his airplane toward the geological feature. As he neared the mountain, he pulled up on the ultralight's stick to follow the ground's contour upward. When he got closer, he spotted a shimmering band of something, like a vertical stripe on the big hill. It took him a moment but he finally realized he was looking at a high waterfall. He flew past the spectacular natural feature, the haze of water droplets forming a rainbow as the sun rose higher in the sky. He looked past the haze to the land itself, trying to make out its ground-level features. He thought he saw what looked like a game trail—a very narrow path—winding its way up, but he couldn't be certain.

He was in the process of turning the ultralight around to make another pass when he heard a high-pitched beeping come from his dashboard.

An alarm.

What?! Antonio's gaze roved over his instrument console, where a red light blinked frantically. As he watched, two more joined the first, along with another alarm, this one low and buzzing. The needles on his gauges began spinning around nonsensically. But he forced himself to stay calm, summoning his inner pilot, and using logic to make sense of the situation. The plane itself was fine, Antonio decided. The thrum of the motor was nice and constant, sounded good. Rather than relying on the fuel gauge, he physically turned around in his seat and looked at the fuel tank—just a large plastic gas can, really—and noted the liquid sloshing around inside. Plenty left. The prop was spinning, the wings and tail were intact…*It's just the electronics, they've gone haywire.*

He could think of no good reason for this, had never experienced anything like it before, nor did he have time to figure it out right now.

The plane dipped left as he neared the waterfall, which created a chaotic swirl of air currents around it. *Geez, watch it, will you!* He admonished himself while righting the craft. His new course put him on parallel flight path with the game trail that looked like it ran right into the waterfall itself. Then he had to veer out of the way of a tall tree that spiked above its counterparts. He slowed the plane to do so, cautioning himself not to cause a stall as he did so. *That's it, easy does it…hey, what's that?*

Down below he got a peekaboo view of a swatch of flat land through the canopy.

And that was when he felt it. A *thunk*. Sort of a low, metallic pinging coming from the chassis of his aircraft. Thinking it was related to the instrument malfunction, he leaned out of the pilot's seat and visually inspected the side of the airplane.

There, wedged in between the frame and his bucket seat, protruded a wooden shaft about four feet long, with bird feathers on one end.

Antonio's adrenaline spiked as the realization dawned on him. An arrow.

Someone was shooting at him.

CHAPTER 3

Antonio's face flushed hot. What to do? He was being shot at! He felt more exposed than ever in his open plane, which was little more than a chair attached to a metal frame with a small motor and a propeller in back. But the good news, if there was any, was that a tribe was nearby. He glanced down but couldn't see any people through the patchwork of green foliage rushing by.

Instinctively, the ecologist banked his plane away from the waterfall and back over the flat jungle. He recalled seeing some kind of open patch down there somewhere and looked for it now, in case he had to make an emergency landing. Who knows what damage the arrow had done, and what if there were more he couldn't see? What if they weren't done shooting and one hits the fuel tank? With these unpleasant thoughts guiding him, Antonio brought his ultralight down until he skimmed just above the rain forest canopy.

There! Through a gap in the trees he glimpsed a barren patch of dirt. If he had to, he could just fit his plane through there...but would there be enough flat ground? It wasn't like he was piloting a 757; he didn't need all that much runway to land his ultralight. But it wasn't a helicopter, either; he needed some room. He started to turn the plane around, to head back for camp, when a volley of arrows flew by the nose of his aircraft, barely missing it. His hand white-knuckled the control stick. He wasn't sure he'd be able to turn around. He pictured his airplane, making the long, lazy circle that a turn necessitated, and the fat, slow target he would present to the archers on the ground.

Then he got another peek at the jungle floor through the trees, a flat inviting expanse of bare dirt. He made his decision. He was going to land. He had no time to second guess his decision. But an opportunity to land this airplane was rare enough out here that he thought he should take advantage of it while he still could. Once he passed the gap in the trees, he might not be able to find it again. At least not before he was shot out of the sky. Or just shot, he reflected grimly, realizing that the only real protection he had was the crash helmet he wore. The rest of his body was almost entirely exposed. If one of those arrows were to hit *him* instead of the plane....

Antonio guided his ultralight lower toward the break in the canopy, seeking the cover it would provide. He was coming in too far to the right and adjusted his course accordingly, being careful not to overcorrect. Visions of his father's wrecked ultralight flashed through his skull and he forced them aside. He'd never had a crash himself, not even close, and he didn't intend to start now.

He felt the barest whisper of leaves brush against the side of his craft as he descended into the jungle. The air instantly became warmer and a little more humid at the same time his surroundings became darker. He pulled off his sunglasses, letting them dangle by the retainer he wore around his neck. He spotted a protruding tree limb up ahead on his right and swerved left, avoiding it. After that he had an unobstructed corridor to the ground, which was smooth enough, but with a jumble of boulders coming up fast straight ahead.

Antonio raised his wing flaps to slow his forward speed. He jostled around in his seat with the sudden correction, hand gripping the stick as the ground rushed up to meet him. This close to it, he could see that it was far from actually being level, but it would have to do as he was far past the point of no return now. An exposed tree root made him worry the landing gear was going to snag it before touching down, but he yanked up on the stick and cleared it with inches to spare. The ground rushed up at a slight incline and his head jolted forward as the plane contacted the ground.

The wheels bounded along at first, the plane hopping while Antonio prayed he wouldn't dig a wingtip into the jungle floor that would send him cartwheeling into a tree trunk. But the little ultralight coasted along until Antonio knew it was under control, that he only needed to apply the brakes in order to stop before he smashed into the jumble of rocks coming up. He applied pressure to the foot pedal and breathed a sigh of relief as the craft slowed, the jostling becoming less pronounced.

The ultralight coasted to a halt a couple of feet in front of the boulders, the prop still spinning as the motor wound down. Antonio tipped his head back against his seat and stared up at the canopy, watching a few leaves flutter down to the forest floor.

He had made it.

He threw off his helmet and picked up his radio transmitter. He raised the technician at his camp's comm tent and told him he had just landed, giving him GPS coordinates. He said he had made contact with a tribe that appeared to be hostile, but now that he was on the ground he was hoping to approach them peacefully and see if they could communicate.

Then he climbed out of his plane and looked around. No people anywhere yet that he could tell. He circled around his ultralight, giving it a quick inspection. Other than the single arrow he'd already seen, everything appeared to be fine. He carefully pulled the arrow from the framework of his plane—fortunately, it was merely wedged in between two struts and not actually embedded into the structure. He examined it closely, marveling at the craftsmanship, at the obvious care and thought that had gone into making this weapon, this tool of survival. The wooden shaft was smooth enough to have come from a lathe, the fletching, or bird plumage secured in place with tree resin. The notch on the end, and the arrow point, a chiseled stone, filed to a razor sharp point that Antonio had no doubt was capable of causing grave damage to human or animal alike.

He heard a voice—not a word but a grunted syllable-- and looked up from the arrow to see three tribal warriors standing on the edge of the clearing, the one in the middle aiming a long spear at him while the two flanking him aimed large bows fitted with arrows of the same type he had just pulled from his plane.

Antonio dropped the arrow and slowly raised his hands above his head in the universal gesture of surrender. He was a little nervous, naturally, but wasn't truly worried yet. He'd had many tribal encounters over the years and, while not an expert on indigenous peoples, was more comfortable than most outsiders when it came to dealing with them. It was common sense really, he told his friends who knew nothing about his line of work. You don't act threatening, be cool, they will treat you the same way, language barrier or no. It was usually when people tried to exploit them or their land that things turned ugly.

And yet, in spite of that, he couldn't help but feel that something was different here. The outward aggression, for one thing. He'd flown over tribes before, many times, and not once had he ever been shot at. Could this be related to the strange incidents he was investigating on behalf of the president?

But then there were the people themselves. The tribesmen aiming their weapons at him. Not typical. It wasn't unusual for them to carry weapons, to make it known that they have them and are prepared to use them if need be, but most tribes did not come out shooting. What had he done to them to provoke such a response?

He hoped to find out without anyone getting hurt. Especially him.

"Hello! I am friend!" he said in Portuguese. When that got no response, he tried again, in Spanish this time. Still no change in demeanor from his jungle hosts. He tried English just for the heck of it, but that, too, had no effect.

Then the trio of tribal men slowly advanced on him, maintaining their weapons-at-the-ready posture. Again, they grunted at him but spoke no actual words in any language that Antonio could make out, even the tribal ones he had become familiar with over the years.

Then there was the appearance of the people. Unlike other tribes he'd come into contact with, they showed absolutely zero modern influence—no Western clothing, jewelry or accessories of any kind. Granted, Antonio thought, this was only three individuals—he had yet to see the rest of the tribe—but still, the face and body paint they wore was different, too, as well as their tattoo patterns and even the ink they used, by the looks of it. In addition, they were fully naked, wearing not even loincloths. Their facial features and jet black hair matched that of other tribal people, but everything else was different.

As the men cautiously approached him, animal-like in their movements and overall deportment, Antonio had a striking thought. He had heard the rumors over the decades, participated in discussions both formal and informal-- in academic conferences and jungle town bars. Talk of uncontacted Amazonian tribes. Jungle people so reclusive and reticent, so resistant to modern ways that they still had yet to have any meaningful interaction with modern society. Sure, it was impossible in this day and age not to have at least seen an airplane passing overhead at some point, or to have found a piece of trash washed up on a river bank, even here, this deep into the rain forest. But for whatever reason, even with these clues that a larger, different world lay beyond the confines of the jungle, there were a handful of tribes, both in the Amazon and around the world, that for whatever reason still live essentially as they had thousands of years ago. For all intents and purposes, they remained uncontacted.

Could these people be from one of those tribes? Antonio flashed on his position, on what he'd done to get here. First of all, his base camp was already deep in the jungle by most people's standards. Just getting to their jumping-off point of the jungle city of Manicoré required a small, private plane flight from the international airport at Manaus, and then there was the three-day jeep ride from Manicoré, plus the one-day hike. That was to base camp. Then from there, just to reach the contacted tribes, it was another half-to-full day's hike deeper into the jungle. And to here…he mentally envisioned his ultralight passing over the mountain with the waterfall and then dropping into the crack in the thick canopy…Another half-day's ultralight aircraft ride.

Goosebumps rose on his arms and legs as the adrenaline spurted through him. *It is possible, isn't it? I really am deep enough into the jungle. I've never been here before, either, to this very place…*With this realization came fear. He felt it now, of that there could be no doubt. The uncontacted tribes were known to exhibit violence at the slightest provocation, or even no provocation other than territoriality, as he had witnessed firsthand in the air today. In general, clashes between all tribes and farmers and agricultural interests were reported with regularity over the years.

But even though the danger was undeniable, contact with an unknown tribe like this represented something else to Antonio: professional advancement. He salivated at the opportunity to be the first researcher to document an uncontacted tribe. Did he bring his camera with him? Not the good one, it was too bulky for the ultralight, but he did have the little point-and-shoot job in the right side pocket of his cargo pants…And the plane's camera! Hopefully it caught the aerial interaction. But then he recalled how all the electronics went haywire. He'd have to check on that later. Right now there were more pressing issues to worry about.

One of the men with a bow and arrow gestured angrily at Antonio's plane, then pointed up to the sky, then to Antonio himself. Antonio nodded. *Yes, it was me.* "I mean no harm," he said in Portuguese, then in Spanish. But the men, all three of them, seemed not to be listening to him at all. They were preoccupied with the ultralight. The one with the spear stayed to guard Antonio while his two compatriots moved cautiously to the aircraft, as if they didn't trust it at all. It wasn't as if it could conceal another person, Antonio thought, so they were probably just curious, never having seen one before up close.

After looking over the plane carefully, without touching it, the two men rejoined their companion who still stood guard over Antonio. The tribal men spoke to each other rapidly in their local dialect, of which Antonio understood exactly none. After this consultation, the one with the spear made eye contact with Antonio and said a single syllable word while pointing towards the base of the mountain. At this the two other tribesmen started to walk, looking behind them to make sure Antonio was going to follow.

He didn't know for sure where they were taking him, but could only assume it was their village, or at least camp, if they were farther from home. The primitive men moved fast, not seeming to run, and yet Antonio had to jog to keep up with them. When they reached the face of the mountain, they turned onto a game trail that hadn't been visible more than a few feet away.

CHAPTER 4

Decha Harutyunyan and Kamnan Mammadov clung to their life raft in the face of strong six-foot waves and howling winds. Having been caught in a sudden gale the previous day off the coast of their native village near Phuket, Thailand, the pair of Thai fishermen had drifted through the night without food or water in their tiny open boat. Given the severity of the storm that had inflicted itself on their old, rusty fishing vessel, they were lucky to be in this position.

Although used to plying the waters of the Andaman Sea, they knew they had been blown far off course for nearly a full day, and now had no idea where they were. They possessed not a single navigational aid between them, and although on a clear night they would be able to take a bearing based on the constellations of stars, right now it was a gray, stormy day that offered no such help.

Both men were lank and skinny even under normal circumstances, and now even more so. Kamnan, the taller of the two, raised his head from where he had been resting it on the rail of the boat, a conscious effort. Through the driving rain, he spotted a form materializing through the gloom. He pointed to it and grunted to gain his companion's attention.

Decha, who had been lying on his back asleep, slowly sat up and followed Kamnan's point with his gaze. His eyes widened.

A landmass.

They had no idea what it was, whether the fates had been kind enough to wash them back home, or if they were hundreds of miles away. But Decha doubted it could be their home. Their fishing vessel had been a hundred miles out to sea already when the trouble had hit. Plus a full day of lifeboat drifting....

But right now he didn't care where it was. Land was land. Their rickety little craft wouldn't hold up forever; as it was they had to constantly bail water out by cupping their hands together and scooping it up and over the side. It was mostly rain water, but even so...eventually the rain and ocean waves would combine to swamp the boat and they would be lost. So this land represented nothing less than salvation.

If they could get to it.

They had one wooden paddle between them. It was the only object in the boat other than the shorts and T-shirts they wore. Fortunately, the wind was blowing toward the land, because they would have never been able to paddle against it the several miles to the island. But with the aid of the howling gusts, Decha was able to use the paddle as a rudder to steer their lifeboat in the right direction and keep them on course. In this manner, hours went by, with the island seeming to grow larger in imperceptible measures. But finally, when it became clear that they were really there, that they had reached land and needed only to navigate the treacherous reef that separated the angry sea from the calm lagoon that fronted the island's palm-fringed beach, Kamnan stood in the boat and pointed the way for Decha to steer.

As he peered into the driving mist, he shook his head. He could see no signs of humanity, no buildings, no people or even signs of people such as boats on the beach. The island appeared to be uninhabited. Even a deserted island represented a huge step up from their current situation, though, so they aimed their little boat toward a break in the reef and hoped for the best.

The passage through the cut in the reef was treacherous and made worse by crashing waves. The flimsy lifeboat couldn't withstand the rigors, and the tiny craft was dashed apart on the razor sharp corals. The two fishermen were washed across the reef until they rolled to a stop, hardly alive, on a tidal flat connected to the island. They lay there for a time, breathing in, breathing out, barely conscious and staring up at the sky, happy to be on solid, if wet, ground.

When they had rested enough, Decha rose to his feet first and roused his friend. They were very parched now, and hungry as well. They knew their ship would be looking for them, along with the Indian Coast Guard, but with the poor weather, there was no telling when or if they would be able to track them to this seemingly desolate island, wherever it was. They staggered across the mud flats, seeking the best place to access the actual island, which they could see now featured a lush jungle backing the sandy beach.

They had reached the edge of the flat, where the ground sloped down to an underwater lagoon, only a short swim separating them and dry land, when an arrow dropped into the mud not two feet in front of them with a wet sucking sound. Decha and Kamnan scanned the beach but saw no signs of people. They made the mistake of casting their gaze back to the arrow and examining it, noting how it was not of modern construction, but hand crafted from all natural materials. *Tribal.*

And that's when a curtain of arrows flew from the jungle in a well-aimed arc, peppering the mud to their left, a staccato rain of wooden shafts that started left of them but before they could move, caught up with Kamnan, who stood on the left. These were thick arrows, about four-feet long, and one of them pierced Kamnan high on the chest, just below his left shoulder, piercing all the way through so that the stone arrowhead protruded from his back. He was spun around violently by the impact, and then staggered to his knees as a second arrow impaled his right shin.

Decha threw his hands in the air as a dozen tribal natives ran out onto the beach, naked but for the simplest of loincloths, skin tattooed and hair decorated with various plant parts. Eight of them stopped at the water's edge, bows and arrows poised, aimed right at the two intruders, while the other four easily waded out to the mud flat.

Decha remained still, hands high in the air while the locals walked up onto the flat. Mortified, he watched as the tribal people jammed arrows into the mud, tail first, and then hoisted his dead friend's body up, holding it high over the arrow tips. They let it drop and the body impaled itself on the arrow tips. Satisfied, the warriors nodded to one another before looking out to sea, and then back to Decha. They nodded to him and pointed back to the island. They said a word to him but he could not comprehend it.

He understood the arrow tip thrust toward his throat though, and proceeded to move as instructed, flanked by a warrior on each side. Terrified, he had no choice but to march on. He was being taken prisoner by this tribe, a native people he had never seen before. Where was he? Taking one last look back toward the mud flat, he saw Kamnan's body silhouetted against the gray sky, and then it hit him: they were leaving him there to rot as a warning to other sailors who might consider landing on these inhospitable shores. *Keep away from this place.*

As he waded at arrow point across the shallow water separating the flats from the beach, staring into the dense jungle that loomed ahead, he couldn't help but wonder.

What would his own fate be?

CHAPTER 5

Brazilian Amazon

Antonio's senses were on high alert as the game trail led into a stand of vegetation so dense it was like walking through a tunnel. He and his tribal escorts (he preferred to think of them that way as opposed to *guards*, at least, even though he was well aware that's what they were) had to duck in places, so low was the green roof. But when the tunnel ended, it emptied into a crater-like natural amphitheater, one that held a village.

The scientist paused at the entrance to this amazing place, wanting to take a moment to assess it, to drink in the details so that he could reflect on it later. But the tribesmen on either side of him pushed him into the amphitheater, where several people nearby—all nearly naked—turned to gawk at him. So much activity, Antonio thought. There had to be at least a hundred people in here, bustling about, coming and going, preparing food, washing utensils and fabrics, working with stone tools and weaponry. There were huts, too, simple ones, some in the middle of the open space, with others lining the perimeter.

Looking straight across the bowl-like area, Antonio could see a rock wall that he knew was the face of the mountain he had flown over earlier. Looking up, a lattice of greenery enshrouded the place, no doubt concealing it from the air. He wanted to stand there and take it all in for longer, but it was too late. A throng of natives surrounded him and began shouting excitedly. It was clear they didn't come into contact with outsiders very often, or at least have them in their village. It made Antonio a little nervous. These people were very far removed from civilization. In fact, he began to suspect that his earlier suppositions were correct, that this tribe may actually be heretofore uncontacted.

Incredible! The scientist in him couldn't help but continue to make observations even as his own personal predicament continued to unfold. Some of the children were tugging at his clothing now, the very texture of it a novelty for them. Others, adults, reached out and felt his hair, running their fingers through it, expressions a mixture of curiosity and mirth.

"Wait, let me show you something! I have something for you!" Antonio said in Portuguese, but he had no doubt the language might as well have fallen on deaf ears. He struggled to recall the word for "gift" he'd used successfully with the known tribes, latching on to it after a few seconds before it could slip away.

He said it, but still received no reaction that suggested recognition. No, he decided, this tribe is speaking not only a different tribal dialect than the ones he'd visited before, but most likely an entirely different language. *Unbelievable!* He couldn't wait to be the one to publish this finding in a scientific journal. A new Amazonian language! He'd be cited by other scholars for decades to come based on that alone, never mind the additional findings that would come from describing the customs and ways of life of this newly discovered culture.

But he was getting ahead of himself. Right now, there were more practical matters to attend to. Looking around the village again, he didn't see any signs of foul play or serious illness or anything else that would cause mass deaths such as those reported in the jungle cities. But he hadn't yet communicated with them about anything, much less the deaths, and that was not going to be a trivial matter.

Antonio took advantage of a small scuffle that broke out among the children who were jockeying for position in order to grope at the outsider, and he slipped a couple of feet away to give him enough space to gesticulate to the elders.

"Okay?" he said, while pointing around the village. He knew that "okay "was high on the list of all the English words recognized by those who didn't speak English. And yet, the only thing the natives seemed to respond to were his physical actions. He winced as the wooden shaft of a spear came down hard on the elbow of his outstretched arm, knocking it down. A stern warning. It dawned on Antonio that he had communicated nothing to these people except perhaps some vague intention of doing harm by pointing.

He made up his mind then and there that, barring some unforeseen developments, he had done what he could and would have to call it a day. It was time to let his camp know that he had made contact with what is likely an unknown tribe, that nothing along the lines of what President Rocha was looking for is showing up here, and then he would return to base camp.

He slowly—very slowly, aware that all eyes were on him—reached into one of his pockets, and removed his digital camera. Upon seeing the shiny metal object, a dozen pair of hands shot out to touch it, but Antonio held it above reach while he powered it on. At the electronic chime and the mechanical whir of the lens opening, the tribal people shrunk back in shock, eyes wide.

"It's okay," Antonio kept repeating in a soothing tone, as if talking to a pack of dangerous animals. He didn't think of them that way, but he had no other way to communicate for the time being. He snapped a picture with the camera and the flash went off, clearly visible and stabbing through the dim shade of the canopied village. The villagers gasped and shielded their eyes. Before any kind of physical reprisal could come, Antonio turned the screen around so that they could see the image he had taken, and the tribal people gaped with wonder at their own likenesses displayed on the device.

"A picture, that's you, I took a picture!" he said in Spanish. As they mobbed in to grab it, Antonio realized his mistake. He would never be able to get that back from them, and now he wouldn't have it to document them with. He did not carry a cell-phone, which might have offered a camera.

The idea was to give them enough gifts for them to be happy with him, so that he may then depart peacefully. Then he would return later with a full expedition to pursue his formal studies.

As he produced a simple Bic lighter, demonstrated how it worked to stunned tribespeople, and then tossed it to them, Antonio backed away from the small mob in order to give himself space to think. He would have to be very careful about who he brought along on this expedition. His current team, while they could certainly be part of it, did not possess sufficient expertise to handle the documentation of an uncontacted human tribe. Not many people in the world did. So who to enlist?

The answer hit him as he watched a man with an animal bone through his nose set fire to a stick using the lighter. He needed an anthropologist. And not just any anthropologist—a couple of the post-docs on his current team were anthropologists, after all, but he required someone with real authority and unparalleled expertise. Antonio himself, as an ecologist, wouldn't be wholly qualified to elucidate the customs and language of these people and place them in proper anthropological context. Then, as he watched the stick burn down to a charred nub while the tribespeople passed it and the lighter back and forth, a name popped into his head, and he knew that was the answer as surely as he knew he was onto something with this strange and primitive tribe.

Stel Foster. "Dr. Stel Foster," he could mentally hear the man say, introducing himself many years ago at a conference on indigenous peoples. "I'm an anthropologist, I study *people,"* he had actually felt the need to point out to Antonio, who understood the reason why. It was because renowned anthropologist Stel Foster, an Englishman educated at and now employed as a researcher by Oxford, was critical of Antonio's own work, and found it to be dismissive of tribal people. He put this disdain into words at that very first meeting of theirs, at what was to be the beginning of a long and bitter rivalry between the two scientists for dominance in rain forest research circles.

"You simply cannot treat indigenous people as bio-cogs in an ecological wheel. They are human beings, and they need to be considered—and treated—as such."

Antonio had defended himself by saying that he studied ecosystems as a whole, and since indigenous tribes were a part of that whole, that made them part of his purview.

Antonio quickly patted down his cargo pants pockets, aware that for the moment he was not under the watchful eyes of his minders while they played with the toys he'd given them. Although he had no cellular, he did have a satellite phone. It was supposed to be for emergency use only, if they needed to call in serious outside help due to a medical emergency, or were they to become dangerously lost, something like that.

But this was a professional opportunity of a lifetime, and he wasn't going to let it pass. He fumbled the phone out, about the same size as a smart-phone, and powered it on, turning so that he faced away from the tribe, lest they see it and want to play with it before he could get his call out. He lit the thing up and opened his contacts, praying that he had remembered to synch his work contacts with this thing. *Come on, come on... There!*

He scrolled through the entries and breathed an audible sigh of relief when he saw *Foster*. The natives were literally getting restless, Antonio thought, knowing that they wouldn't be distracted for much longer.

He tapped the screen and placed a call to his professional rival.

CHAPTER 6

Andaman Islands, Indian Ocean

Dr. Stel Foster's mouth turned down at the corners as he thanked the ship's communications officer. They were almost to the island, and so he wondered who would be placing a shore-to-ship call for him now. Hopefully not the Indian government, who had sent him on this voyage. There had been an increase of late in reports of violent clashes between a notorious native tribe of the islands and passing fishermen and other boaters. Better make sure, though, Stel thought, moving from his place against the ships rail, where he'd been getting his first good glimpses of the Andamans. Lush jungle, mostly flat interior, beaches and mud flats.

The last thing he needed was to come all this way for nothing, but it would be even worse if he were to actually go through the trouble of getting off the ship and making landfall on the island before he found out something went wrong with the funding. He was not one to work for free or to waste his time. If this turned out to be a wild goose chase, then fine, but he had other things to do, no need to hang around here.

He breezed into the communications room, although he found "room" to be a little grandiose a term for the small alcove tucked away in the bridge. But it did have a working ship-to-shore phone and a communications officer manning it. That man nodded at his approach and handed him the receiver. "For you, sir, caller says it's urgent." He cupped a hand over the mic, in case Foster refused the call.

"Where are they calling from, New Delhi?"

The comm man shook his head. "Brazil, sir."

Brazil? Now that was strange. "I'll take it."

The ship's officer handed him the mic and left the alcove, drawing the curtain across as he did so. As if that did anything, Foster thought. All it did was give the illusion of privacy, anyone on the bridge could still hear perfectly well what was being said. But he knew he was being cynical, as always. The curtain was to cut down on the bright light through the bridge windscreen in daylight, which made it hard to read the radio displays.

Foster sat on the stool that was bolted to the deck and held the receiver to his ear. "Dr. Stel Foster speaking, to whom do I have the pleasure of interrupting my science cruise for?"

But even before the caller, whoever it was, began speaking, Stel knew this call was going to be interesting. In the background he heard wild shouting, or enthusiastic grunts, or some combination of it. Very tribal, that was for certain. For a moment he thought someone was playing back one of his many field recordings he'd made *in situ* of tribal people over the course of his career. Except that it couldn't be. The voices grew louder, and he was able to make out individual words. Except they weren't words he understood, and that's what made it so very odd. Because he was an expert in tribal linguistics. As close to fluent as any non-indigenous person could be. And yet....

I have no idea what those people are saying. Putting it down to some kind of prank, he decided to get on with the call. He had imminent business to attend to here, after all. "Am I the only one on my end of the party line here? Anyone going to talk to me?"

There was a beat and then a male voice, American, came on the line. "I'm not sure that even the likes of you would be able to converse with these people. And in that context, it's good to talk to you, Stel."

Stel racked his brain to match a face to the voice, and then he got it.

UNCONTACTED

That wanker American, the *ecologist*. Always trying to one-up him in the journals. "Antonio? Is that you? Where are you?"

"It's me, Stel. I'm in the Amazon, and I've found something here you're going to want to see."

37

CHAPTER 7

Brazilian Amazon

Antonio ended the sat-phone call and pocketed his device as the tribespeople tugged him back into the thick of things, into the center of the village circle. They wanted to show him a few things now, including a selection of animal hides, bones, teeth, and jewelry fashioned from the same. They foisted upon him a feathered necklace made from the plumage of parrots. Antonio tried to tell them that a trade wasn't necessary for the items he had given them, but this was impossible to convey and he certainly didn't want to insult them by refusing what they had to offer, so he accepted and put it around his neck.

After trading a few more items, Antonio pointed to one of the huts, constructed from thatched palm fronds interwoven with bamboo, trying to hint that he wanted to go inside one. If nothing else it would give him additional insights into this tribe's way of life. Surprisingly, they readily agreed, and he was soon encircled by tribe-members of all ages as they walked him to one of the huts near the center of the village circle.

A curtain of vines hung over the doorway, and one of the villagers held them aside as Antonio stepped through. Inside, a light and pleasant fragrance issued from a pile of sticks and leaves burning in a stone bowl near the center of the hut, which had only a dirt floor covered with woven grass mats. Three people occupied this space, all of them elderly females, and all of them sitting cross-legged on the floor and weaving more mats out of palm leaves. Antonio nodded at them and they stared at him without nodding in return or saying anything.

Antonio exited the hut and he was then led to another next to it, this one occupied by four men sharpening arrow points on a smooth, large stone. One of the men held up a point he had been working on and held it out to Antonio. When he hesitated, the tribal man, also somewhat elderly in appearance, although Antonio supposed that could mean he was somewhere in his forties, wobbled the arrowhead in his palm and leaned in close to Antonio. The ecologist reached out and took the weapon. He was surprised by its heaviness, and again by the sharpness of its sides. Modern manufactured arrowheads made from metal had nothing on this finely crafted implement, Antonio thought. He handed the arrowhead back to the craftsman, wondering if one of these four men had made the arrow point that had struck his ultralight.

He thanked them as best he could for their hospitality and was shown out of the hut and around to more of them, repeating much the same scenes of domesticity or craftsmanship. When he had visited all of the central huts he looked over to the largest perimeter structure, an elongated lodge-type building with large open-air windows running most of its length. Standing at one of the windows and observing him was an older tribesman. Antonio was about to point him out as a way of asking who he was, that is, what was his job in the tribe. Maybe they'd let him tour that building, too, who knew?

But then the children mobbed him again, this time fixating on his watch. he was prepared to barter it if need be, so he unlatched it from his wrist. When he handed it over to a small sea of outstretched hands, he caught the time on it one final time. He was surprised to learn that hours had passed since he'd landed. Looking up into what sky peeked through the canopy, he could tell it would be dark soon. It was time to make contact with his team.

With his wristwatch in the hands of the children, some of the pressure was off of him as the tribe passed around the foreign gadget, and so Antonio stepped a few feet away toward two of his minders, as he thought of them, that he recognized from his welcoming committee at his plane's landing site. He conveyed to them through hand signals that he needed to return to his plane, and then pantomimed using the radio, which they had seen him do before.

He wasn't sure what their reaction would be, but was surprised to be met with immediate agreement. Sure, they seemed to say, let's go. It concerned him a little that they wouldn't let him go alone, though, but then again he wasn't trying to escape. Quite the opposite, he was trying to contact his own people to tell them he'd be staying here longer under his own volition. He set off down the path outside the village with a contingent of tribal minders.

Once at the ultralight, Antonio was mildly amused, but also concerned, to see a small monkey scuttle out of the frame upon hearing their approach. He had no doubt that were his aircraft to remain here indefinitely (such as if he died in the jungle), that the rain forest would claim the ultralight as its own, overgrowing it, raining it to rust and burying it in leaf litter until it no longer remained in its present form, sort of like a shipwreck that succumbs over the years to the ocean. Explorers in some distant decade would come across it, document it, and speculate as to how it came to be.

But although he could visualize that process, the presence of a single monkey and a few leaves on his seat were a far cry from rendering his craft inoperable. Antonio moved to the flight radio, basically a handheld air band transmitter zip-tied to the dash, and broadcast a greeting to his team's communications tent.

He was both surprised and pleased to hear Richards' voice answer.

"Good to hear from you, mate. Was getting a bit worried. What's your status?"

Antonio eyed the natives, who had drawn their bows in response to the radio voice belonging to an unseen human, no doubt a spirit of some sort to their minds. His only consolation was that he could communicate with Richards without any fear of the natives understanding what was being said.

"Richards, I've made quite the discovery here. I've come into contact with a tribe that is extremely primitive."

"Well aren't they all?" He guffawed over the speaker and the natives wore perplexed expressions as they slowly circled around the front of the plane, weapons still drawn.

"Not like this. Richards, I think this tribe has never before been contacted. By anyone."

"What? Come on, man. What makes you think that?"

"The language, for one thing, the fact that they have exactly zero modern items in their possession, for another, and their reaction to seeing me and my belongings for a third."

"What about the actual reason for the visit—anything along the lines of what the president was looking for?"

"Negative. It all seems like normal tribal life, not that I'm able to communicate with them as well as the other tribes we've visited. But the real excitement here is the tribe itself."

"Antonio, if what you're saying turns out to be true--"

"It's huge! I know! Think of the papers, enough to last the rest of our careers…"

"We'll need outside corroboration."

"Way ahead of you." Antonio detailed his call with Stel Foster.

"That jackass, huh?"

"He knows what he's doing though, Richards, more than we do, you have to admit."

"I know. Well, maybe we'll get lucky and he'll turn it down. You haven't heard back from him yet, right?"

"Right. We'll see. I know he's not the only anthropologist on the planet, but he's my first choice. This is too potentially monumental to screw up."

"So it's almost dark. I take it you'll be staying with your new friends tonight?"

Antonio looked up again at the warriors, all three of which were running their fingers over the paint that comprised the plane's serial number on the tail, as if mystified that it didn't smudge. "That's the plan."

"I know I don't have to tell you this, old friend, but be careful, okay?"

"Of course. How are things on your end? You guys find any more tribes?"

"One more. We made contact with the Matsés, but they all seem fine, too. We spoke with them in their own dialect and the last death they had was about a year ago, a woman who drowned in the river after a hard rain while doing laundry."

"All right, so let's move on from this, then. Go ahead and contact the president and let him know that we've made contact with a number of tribes—including one at the coordinates I radioed earlier."

"Better give them to me again, just to be sure."

Antonio leaned over and squinted at the radio display to read the numbers there from the integrated GPS. He recited them to Richards.

"Good stuff. So listen, Antonio—I'll carry on our regular research here as planned until you get back, but if you need us to, we could make the trek."

"Copy that. I'll radio tomorrow, breakfast time."

Antonio turned off the radio, fully realizing that the very last thing he needed was to have some piece of electronics left on overnight, drain out the plane's battery and be unable to start the engine in the morning. After double-checking that everything was off, he signaled to his warrior escorts that he was ready to return to camp. He wasn't sure exactly what was going to happen when it came to time actually leave, if they would try to stop him, but for now, he felt like he was doing the right thing.

As they walked along the narrow game trail that would take them back to the village, he thought about the things he should try to observe and take mental notes of, things that would help formulate a more formal research plan, especially if Foster came on board. Then a vine caught him off guard as he was wondering how long it was take his rival to get back to him. These kinds of thoughts kept him mentally occupied until they reached camp as dusk fell.

A large fire burned in the center of the village now, as well as a few torches around the perimeter. Antonio would have thought the flames would have given their presence away by now, but looking up and seeing the heavy foliage cover, as well as the mountain wall blocking all view from one side, he understood how they had remained hidden. Not only that, he mused, looking around the settlement, he doubted they had lived here forever. These huts weren't that difficult to build, they could probably move around when the need arose. That was something else he wanted to ask them about that was beyond his ability to communicate, so he filed it away for later.

Looking around the village, he glanced over at the longer huts, sort of like the longhouses the known tribes built, but a little different in style, more open Antonio noticed. Scanning along the length of one of the ones he hadn't yet been inside, he saw the same older man he'd seen earlier, peeking out at him. He wondered what his role was in the camp. The big buildings—did they connote the importance of those who occupied them, or were they merely community structures to accommodate more people? Deciding he needed to find out, Antonio decided to first create a distraction to allow himself a little more privacy.

He fished around in his pockets for a gift the tribe would find interesting that he hadn't yet used. He came up with a small pack of crayons, which had always served him well with the known tribes he'd visited. When the kids and a few adults alike were drawing on each other with them, Antonio walked casually toward the long hut. The tribe was becoming a little more used to him, and he was able to reach the structure without being followed. At least so far. He had no idea how long that would last, but he would make a go of it while he could.

He reached the base of the structure and looked up to see the old man standing in the window again. This time, he waved to Antonio before quickly shrinking out of sight. Antonio couldn't believe it. The gesture was unmistakable—come here! Antonio looked around to see what the rest of the tribe was doing, but they were still preoccupied with the crayons and each other. None of them were even looking his way.

Antonio moved to the nearest entrance to the long hut, a series of simple log steps that led up to the wooden plank floor. He could smell the aroma of the same incense-like fragrance he had smelled in the other hut in here, too, although he couldn't see the source. Besides the old man and Antonio, four other tribe members occupied this room, all of them sitting on the floor and seeming to chant, although they looked up at Antonio's arrival. Looking both left and right down the long hut, other tribal people could be seen in the rooms further down, some sitting, some standing.

The tribal man spoke to Antonio in his language, a rapid fire, chant-like dialect that Antonio still could not comprehend any better than he had when he'd arrived. Again, to show he was trying to communicate, Antonio spoke a few of the words he knew from other tribal dialects, and again, this man couldn't understand him. Only, his reaction was different. The others returned his attempts at conversing in a tribal language with blank stares. But this man, he shook his head. *No.* Antonio thought back to his previous interactions and tried to recall any of the others doing that. He could not.

And then the tribal man was handing him a piece of paper, a wrinkled, dirty, folded piece of paper. Puzzled, Antonio took it and unfolded it. It consisted of one line written, amazingly enough, in English:

THEY ARE GOING TO KILL YOU.

CHAPTER 8

Antonio's mouth dropped open in utter shock and surprise upon reading the note. He looked up at the man who had given it to him, whose eyes now burned into his own, conveying nothing but seriousness. Antonio pointed to the note and asked, in English, "Do you speak English?" Something about his eyes intrigued Antonio. He wore a facial mask of clay or mud, and his hair was caked with some kind of pigmented dirt, making it appear blue rather than the jet black the rest of the natives shared. His body, too, was covered in an earthen mask.

The man suddenly turned and walked away, deeper into the long hut. Antonio glanced briefly around, and seeing no one paying much attention to him, followed.

"Wait! Please?" He called after him in English. The man continued striding away, so Antonio pursued him, increasing his own pace. "Let me talk to you."

They walked through the long hut, the old man leading the way. Antonio recognized a few of the tribe members in the next room he passed though, and though they looked up at him, they quickly went back to what they were doing with their earthenware pots without raising too much interest. Antonio caught up to the man who had given him the note at the end of the last room, which was unoccupied. An open doorway led back out to the village common area, but no one was visible immediately outside the long hut.

The old man stopped and stared at Antonio, who held up the note and snapped it with a finger, before throwing up his hands in a gesture he hoped would be interpreted as a question, as in, Who wrote this?

"Me? Is this for me?" Antonio tried English, not expecting an answer, but hoping his tone conveyed that he sought one.

"We have about two minutes to talk before the others will need this hut to prepare dinner." The man coughed, a wet, productive hacking that he made no effort to hide.

Antonio's jaw dropped open as he looked up from the paper. He'd examined it more closely, front and back, looking for anything he might have missed. But the sound of spoken English caused him to look around. Was there someone else here? He didn't see anyone. Perhaps a radio or some type of loudspeaker somewhere, a tv?

"Antonio, It's starting. I've been expecting you."

Antonio looked back to the man just in time to see his lips stop moving at the end of the sentence. There could be no doubt.

"You speak *English*?"

"And Portuguese. You used to speak Portuguese too, you know, when you were a baby. I tried to get you to keep it up after we moved to the States, but your mother—"

Antonio's brain seemed to melt into itself, to dissolve into what surely must be some kind of hallucinatory dream. Perhaps he'd had some tainted water, or they had slipped him some medicinal herbs without his knowing? Because this was impossible. There was only one person from whom these words made any sense, and that was his…

He couldn't even get himself to think it without almost doubling over, sort of half spinning around, making movement of any kind simply to distract his brain. But there was no way around it. He kept coming back to the same conclusion. And then the tribal man spoke again.

"It's me, Antonio. I always knew you would come."

Antonio studied the face before him, the mud-covered cheeks, the dark blue-green tribal tattoo lines across the eyes and running down the cheekbones, at the matted hair. And then he focused on the teeth, on the upper left incisor, which had a chip out of it. He flashed on his father teaching him to play baseball, and one day, his confidence too high, Antonio had swung the bat mightily but lost his grip, sending the wooden shaft spinning into his father's mouth, chipping the tooth. He'd never had it fixed, claiming it was no big deal, he had better things to spend his time and money on than going to the dentist, and finally, with his trademark sense of humor, that it would serve as a reminder to duck faster next time.

His father.

Antonio held onto the door frame as his knees started to buckle. *"Dad?"*

"Antonio, it's me." He pulled his son close and embraced him for a long moment before pushing him away.

"Dad, what....I thought you--"

"Died in the ultralight crash?"

"Yes, of course!" Antonio flashed on the day, twenty-two years ago, when he got the call that his father had been missing for twenty-four hours and was presumed dead in a Brazilian Amazon field accident. An ultralight plane crash, they'd said. Not survivable, although his body was never found. The frantic search in the days that followed to look for his father, a search that ended in vain.

"But what *happened* to you? How are you still alive? What have you been doing all this time?"

His father leaned in close, his breath now apparent as a raspy wheeze. "I'm sorry to have to tell you this, son, but it wasn't an accident."

Antonio was speechless, with one hand on his father's shoulder and the other on a bamboo pole on the hut's doorway, beyond which a child ran by but didn't linger.

"What do you mean it wasn't an accident, Dad? The plane...I saw it myself, it was so mangled, high in the trees, how could anyone have survived that?"

"I parachuted out right before it hit the trees."

Antonio's mind lit on the details of his father's disappearance, fresh across the years because he'd reviewed the official missing person's case file so many times. *The victim was reported to have been wearing a small backpack as he boarded the ultralight aircraft…*Antonio had spent not an insignificant amount of time over the decades pondering that backpack, because there was no extra room in an ultralight—especially the ones in his father's day—for any extra gear, even a backpack. To wear it would mean you couldn't lean back properly in the pilot's seat. So the fact that he brought one must mean that whatever it contained was most important indeed. Scientific gear, perhaps? He didn't see how accessing it while aloft would be practical or feasible. But now the answer became clear:

A parachute.

That explained it. That would be worth taking along, if one knew they were going to be in a crash, but of course, that meant…

"So you meant to crash the ultralight all along? Why? For Christ's sake, Dad, *why?*"

Antonio was pressed up against his father, now seeing right through the tribal garb to the man himself. The old man coughed again and wiped away phlegm with the back of his hand. Antonio caught sight of bloody globules in the spittle.

"Antonio, all of my research—up to that point in my career, and up to now—was leading me to this place. I knew it was the only way I'd be able to find the truth. By being here. I mean really *being* here, living here amongst the people…" He paused while he looked himself up and down…"by ultimately *becoming* one of these people…"

"What truth, Dad? What truth? Because I sure as hell never got any truth. Not until now, anyway. And this is just so…so random, such an accident. What if I had never found you by accident like this?"

The old man's eyes met his in a powerful gaze. "It's not an accident, son."

Antonio threw up his hands. "What are you talking about? Do you even know why I'm here? If it wasn't' for—"

"Does it have to do with February 29?"

Antonio broke himself off in mid-sentence. A tiger beetle scuttled down the door frame and he watched its progress. How could his father have known about that date?

"So you have a radio here somewhere? You heard the news?"

His father shook his head. "There are no electronics of any kind at this village. They would not be accepted. And if I were to bring them, by extension, *I* would not be accepted."

"Then how did you hear about it?"

His father leaned in even closer after a quick sideways glance, presumably to make sure none of the tribe was observing them. "Every single member of this tribe was born on February 29. They always have been, since time immemorial." He saw the look of incredulity forming on Antonio's face and headed it off. "They keep birth records. One of the few indigenous tribes that does. Why do you think that is?"

Antonio said he didn't know.

"Because they know it's important somehow. Like they were *decreed* to do it, long ago. And I understand you're skeptical, how could you not be? But they have birth records."

"They have written birth records?"

"Yes, for every single member of this tribe. You can ask Guató, later, to show you. Say the words *Tupi-Tenetehara-Cayua* and he will know exactly what you mean. There's a records monument underneath one of the central huts, one you entered today already, and in there are stacks of chiseled tablets with the names and birthdates, all February 29."

Antonio thought about this for a moment. It was not unheard of for primitive tribes to keep birth records, although it was uncommon. "Okay, the birth records I can accept. But how is it possible that all of them were born on the same day? That's simply impossible, statistically. The records must be some kind of hoax, Dad. Kind of like your ultralight accident, right?"

His father stared at him for a long spell, maintaining eye contact. "What's your birthday, Antonio? And mine?"

All of a sudden Antonio's guts tied up in knots. Of course Antonio knew his own birthday. It was February 28. That's what he'd known it as his whole life, that's what was on his driver license, his passport, and every other official document he possessed, including his birth certificate.

Except that it wasn't his real birthday.

He recalled the first conversation he'd had about it with his mother and father, when he was about eight years old. About how he had been born on an unusual birthday, one that only came around every fours years, so instead of a lifetime of inconveniences, of having to celebrate birthdays either a day early or a day late, or being unable to select his birthdate on some computer forms, things like that, his parents took their doctor's suggestion of selecting February 28 on his birth certificate as his date of birth on record. The rest of his life he'd known his own birthday as February 28, 1972, except that it wasn't.

It was February 29, 1972.

He eyed his father. "I have the same birthday as the tribe, is what you're saying."

His father nodded. "And as me."

Inside Antonio felt things click into place. His father did have the same birthday as he did. He remembered the day when, as a teenager, his father had come down from the attic, dusty and sweaty, waving a creased piece of paper in each hand as he barged into Antonio's room. "I found it!"

"Found what?"

"My real birth certificate. It was in a box of things from your grandmother's house. Antonio's grandma had passed away a few months before. It had been the first funeral Antonio had ever been to.

"I thought you already had that."

"I thought I did, too. But look!" He smoothed out the yellowed old paper on young Antonio's homework desk, and next to it placed a newer-looking white one. Both were his birth certificate, but he pointed to the year on the yellow one.

"See that date there?"

Antonio nodded. "February 29, 1940…Hey! We just had your birthday last week, and it was March 1st!"

"That's right, kiddo. All my life I have. I'm just finding this out right now. I think it must be because the hospital made my parents pick a date on either side of it, to avoid clerical and administrative problems."

Antonio took a deep breath before continuing. It was all getting too much to bear, like he could feel a certain truth closing in on him but wasn't sure what it was yet. "You never answered my earlier question: How did you hear about what's happening here in the first place?"

"I became a part of it, that's how." He saw the shocked look forming on his son's face and quickly added, "Not the deaths. They're only a side-effect of what these people have been entrusted with."

Antonio held out the note. "Speaking of deaths what's this about? Your tribe—adopted family, I guess you could say—is going to kill me?"

His father nodded, voice lowering to barely above a whisper. "I'm risking my own life—or what's left of it—" He turned away to cough out more bloody phlegm. "…to warn you. Listen to me, son. There is an object being guarded deep in the jungle by this tribe."

Antonio shrugged. "What object?"

"I'd like to show you. It's impossible to explain. Not only that, son, but I am very ill. It seems that the decades of primal living have caught up to me, and I am sure that I do not have long. Probably only weeks at best. That's why they give me the run of the best hut," he finished, waving an arm around at the simple structure as though it were the Ritz Carlton.

"Okay, where is it?" Antonio looked outside the hut door as though it might be right there.

"it's not far from here, a short hike through the jungle. I can point you the way on the right path, but from there you'll be on your own. I'm not fit enough to make the trek."

"Looks like I'm used to you leaving me on my own, anyway, right?"

His father maintained eye contact and slowly shook his head. "The world is in danger, son. If I hadn't done what I'd done…" He trailed off and shook his head. "Humanity would be done for. So I waited for someone to come along all these years. I figured the odds were good it would be you."

"Fine, show me the way to go see this thing, whatever it is."

"First, I must warn you: the tribe already suspects you are a threat, due to the timing of your appearance. If they find out that you know about the object, they will kill you immediately and without any sort of due process. Crush your head in between the ends of two logs swung through the air on ropes. I've seen it happen to others. I wouldn't be able to stop it." The old man blanched for a moment and swallowed back rising bile.

"Why did you tell me about it then, you idiot?" Antonio felt awful calling his father that, especially after being so long apart, but his anger had the better of him now, being tricked like this, and now subjecting him to some kind of tribal danger.

"Because the world needs to know, Antonio. Everyone will die if we don't know—I mean *everyone*, not just the tribe."

"You said that before. It makes no sense to me."

"Just come with me—quickly!" He looked out of the doorway and then jogged down the six steps to the dirt below. Antonio followed, and his father led him behind the long hut until they were shielded from the village. He broke a stick off of a branch and pointed with it into the jungle, along a large game trail the hunters used daily.

"Listen, son. This is your path. You follow along this path until it forks, and I will draw you the rest." He used the same stick to scratch out lines and shapes in the dirt, with a surprisingly fast and accurate hand for so frail a person. To Antonio it looked like he had just finished and was looking back up from his work when his father gripped his throat and slumped into the dirt.

"Dad, what's the matter—Dad?"

Antonio knelt and pulled his fathers hand away from his neck, straightening him out on the ground, preparing to give him CPR. He felt for a pulse, and felt the last one before it stopped forever. Antonio performed CPR on his father anyway, but he knew it was no use. It was almost as if his father had been expecting this, had been waiting for him to get here so that he could die. He had finally found his father and now he had left him again.

Antonio looked down at the drawing his father had left him and wondered if everything he said could have been the result of delirium. He looked into the dense jungle along the path his Dad had pointed out for him, and then back to the drawing, studying it for a few moments until he was sure he understood it. He wished he could take a picture of it, but he'd foolishly given his camera to the tribe.

He stood and passed his boot across the map before walking around the end of the same hut he'd been inside, to the village circle. He felt exposed, as if all eyes must be on him, but in actuality the tribe was going about their business, some of them still playing with the items he'd given them. He picked up a spear from a rack and pointed to a boar in a crude cage. The natives huddled nearby grinned at him.

Antonio pointed to himself, then to the boar, then to the forest, holding up the spear while he did so. *I go hunt pigs now,* he hoped he was conveying. The tribal men grew wide smiles and laughed to each other, until a couple of them waved their arms in jerky motions toward the jungle. *Yes, go, more boar!*

Antonio nodded to them and moved with his spear and the small pack he wore to the edge of the rain forest.

CHAPTER 9

Andaman Islands, Indian Ocean

Stel Foster grinned as he walked along the rain forest trail, leaving the beach behind. *Antonio Medina, eh? Calling out of the blue with something that sounds interesting. He must really need help if he swallowed his pride enough to call me.* He'd promised Antonio on the call that he would get over to the Amazon. He had another grant to work on there if Antonio's promising lead turned out to be a wild goose chase, so there wasn't much to lose, really. But first he had an obligation to attend to for the Indian government, right here on this very isle.

"Watch it, Alfred!" he called out to his colleague up ahead. "Try to cut that branch off completely if you can, not sure the porters are going to be able to make it under there."

The expedition was small by Dr. Foster's standards. Only himself, his long-time, trusted colleague, Dr. Alfred Algers, also from Oxford, and a pair of Indian porters to carry much of their gear. In addition, there was the boat crew that would remain at anchor off the beach until Stel's party returned.

"Right, mate, got it," Algers called back, and then Stel heard the hacking of a metal blade on wood. The obstacle was cleared out of the way and then the small procession resumed its trek deeper into the interior of this remote, forbidding island. When they reached the top of a grassy rise that afforded a view into a deep, forested valley below, Stel shrugged off his pack and called for a rest break. But before they could relax, he raised a hand in the air, a signal for quiet. Then he crouched and signaled for the others to do the same.

As they watched, a tribal man with black hair and his body painted in solid red, raised a spear above his head. He arched his back as he brought it forward in a thrusting motion. Even from this height, Stel could hear the squeal of the hunter's intended target, followed by the rustle of bushes. Then a small deer ran from the clump of foliage into a small clearing, where it began spinning and kicking wildly, a spear protruding from its right flank. The human was on his prey in an instant. Stel saw a piece of rock glint dully in the tropical sunlight before it came down with a thud on the animal's head. They continued to observe in silence, Algers taking video, while the hunter cleaned and dressed his kill. That done, he then slung his prize over his shoulder and walked away from Stel's party, deeper into the island forest.

Stel and his team visually tracked the warrior until he had disappeared from sight into the forest proper. Stel waved his arm and they descended the hill. Down on flat ground, they carefully picked their way toward where the tribal hunter had disappeared. They passed over the blood-matted grass where the animal kill was made and squeezed through the low brambles, taking cover in their head-high chaos while they watched and listened for the tribal man.

The humidity stifled all, except for the hum of insects that was a constant, droning presence. Stepping over a log, Stel watched a snake—he thought it might be a black mamba—wind itself out from under the wood before it slithered off into a pile of palm fronds. They moved on, all careful now to watch for signs of animal predators as well as tribal presence. This tribe was known to be hostile, and so safety and watchfulness would be key.

#

Safety meant proceeding slowly, and so it was well into the afternoon by the time they were within earshot of the tribal settlement. Not a large one by area or people, Stel figured it was probably one of several neighboring "pods" or contained villages. He was sure there would be a central village somewhere, but for now this outpost would have to do.

It quickly became apparent that the one huge opportunity it did afford was language observance. With silence maintained on the expedition team in order to remain undetected, it was easy to hear individual conversations. Stel leaned in as he silently activated a long-range audio recorder, to capture linguistic samples of the tribe. Once he was sure it was recording and that the levels were good, Stel concentrated on the language itself. At first he thought the sound quality was garbled, because he couldn't make out what they were saying. Which was pretty much impossible, since Dr. Stel Foster knew almost every tribal language on Earth.

The realization struck him like a brick: he really couldn't understand what they were saying. And the reason he couldn't was because their language was previously undocumented, and that could mean only one thing: that this was an uncontacted tribe.

Stel shook his head slowly as he observed the primitive humans, watching them with the naked eye from afar but listening to their conversations through the sensitive microphone. *Unbelievable.* He was aware that on this planet there were maybe a handful of such tribes still hanging on, and he also knew, from previous studies of tribes in this general region where flare-ups occur between the tribe and people from the modern world, that they were a more primitive group than usual. But this....he cocked his head to one side and *shushed* one of the porters as they made noise scuffling their feet to shift positions. This seemed to be an entirely new tribe, smack dab in the middle of the region that he'd never dealt with before. *What a godsend.*

And then a feeling that was hard for him to describe took hold as he recalled his rival's out-of-the-blue phone call, asking him to come to the Amazon. *The second uncontacted tribe in the same day?* It was unthinkable, so beyond mere coincidence that he wanted to think about it extensively, for he knew there must be a—

"*Stel. Stel!*"

Alfred's voice broke him from his thoughts. "Watch, over there." He pointed off to his left and saw four tribal men focusing their attention on a mound of chiseled stones, working or doing something to it. Stel had been so focused on listening to the tribe that he'd forgotten to watch them, to look around.

"What are they doing?"

Alfred fumbled in the pockets of his photography vest until he removed a pair of compact binoculars. He focused them on the activity. "They appear to be removing a stone cap of some sort…wait, hold on…another one of them is bringing a stone tablet, it looks like…they're dropping it into the pit…." He looked up from the binoculars. "What do you think that's all about?" he asked Stel.

"It's got to be either some kind of religious observance or…" He reached out a hand to Alfred. "Let me see the glasses." Alfred handed them over and Stel focused in on the scene. "They seem to be rearranging whatever's in there. More stone tablets. They're now replacing the stone cap." He handed the binoculars back to Alfred, who added, "Religious observance, or what?"

"Or a record keeping system."

Alfred appeared to consider this carefully for a moment. "What kind of primitive—not just primitive, mind you, but so primitive that they're virtually *uncontacted*—tribe keeps written records, about anything?"

"This one, Alfred. This one does, I'd say. But let's go pay them a visit and find out for sure, shall we?"

CHAPTER 10

Brazilian Amazon

The jungle grew very thick only a few meters away from the village, so much so that Antonio had to stop often to snap branches out of the way or clear vines from his path. He wished he had his machete, but he hadn't brought it because it was too much for the ultralight, and even if he had it, it would have been taken from him by the tribe. He hadn't seen any metal objects in their possession at all so far, and had no doubt that they'd want the blade for that reason alone.

After clearing out an area that gave him enough room to stand unmolested by plants, Antonio came upon a fork in the path. He mentally pictured the crude map his father had drawn in the dirt. *Just before he died*. He zoomed in on it with his mind's eye, a peanut gallery of exotic birdcalls his only soundtrack while he concentrated. After a short time he could picture it clearly, as if he was standing in the dirt right beside it.

He moved off accordingly, to his left, toward the green cliff. If anything the vegetation grew even thicker the closer he got to the wall, but he kept moving. After a while he heard the sound of rushing water. Falling water, he realized, picturing the waterfall he'd seen on his aerial pass on the way in here. He moved toward the sound. The ground grew damper the closer he got, spray from the waterfall coating everything, including Antonio himself.

He heard a rustling off to his right, and swiveled his head in time to see some sort of small mammal dart off into the underbrush. It occurred to him that he was supposed to be on a hunting trip, and that if he could actually come back with some game it would bolster his story greatly. So far he had used the spear he had made a show of taking only as a walking stick. He was under no illusion that catching a wild animal in that manner would be easy, though. He'd never tried it himself, although he'd seen it done more than once by tribespeople. Still, maybe he would get lucky, he thought, and so he ducked under some branches and moved away in the direction in which the animal had gone.

After a few steps he glanced left, right, and then right again, but saw nothing. Only a few seconds had passed since he'd seen the beast, and he didn't see how it could have moved beyond his sight yet. He looked straight ahead and caught the slightest movement—the leaves on the end of a branch bouncing ever so slightly. He took three more steps in that direction and then froze.

The ground opened up in what could be called either a large burrow or a small tunnel. It descended gradually beneath the earth at a walkable angle, although Antonio would have to stoop to pass through. Clearly that's where the animal had gone.

Antonio walked to the edge of the opening and peered inside. He pictured his father's map again, and it dawned on him that this feature could be that one strange line he had questioned earlier, something that hadn't seemed right but when viewed in person, as an underground feature it made perfect sense.

Was this what his father was bringing him to? He wasn't about to go down there after an animal, but for whatever it was his Dad had wanted him to see…He crouched lower and gazed into the tunnel, wondering how far it went. Picturing the map yet again, if his assumption was correct about that part of it representing subterranean avenues, then it should be extensive and not merely a cul-de-sac style animal burrow.

He wished he had a flashlight, but he'd given the one small one he'd taken along to the tribe, who were no doubt still amazing themselves with it at this very moment. Deciding he would explore the tunnel to the extent that daylight penetrated, the scientist lowered his head and duck-walked into the subterranean opening.

CHAPTER 11

Antonio cursed softly to himself as he lost his footing in the loose mud of the confined space. Even though his eyesight was adjusting to the dim light, it was still very dark in here and he questioned how much farther he would be able to go without artificial light or at least a torch, of which he had neither.

He descended deep into a complex labyrinth of crisscrossing tunnels, and before he knew it, the darkness was almost absolute and he had to look back to see any light at all. Turning back around to face the blackness ahead of him, he wished he had some equipment. He wasn't afraid of caves or being underground. As an ecologist, he'd done his PhD dissertation on bats in Costa Rica, and as part of that research he had ventured deep into their underground lairs to observe their habits. Since then, he'd been underground many times, which was why he was okay with what he was doing now. But without equipment, he had real limits. He wasn't foolhardy. At a bare minimum, a light source and guidance system, like a simple spool of rope to pay out as he progressed inside, were necessary to avoid getting lost and wandering in the dark, bumping into walls until he blacked out from thirst and starvation.

Aware of these dangers, he was preparing to turn around when a faint sparkle caught his eye. Ahead and to his left. A glowing that was steady with no pulse. As he watched, it maintained its brightness and he was able to fix its position. Hands out in front of him in case he should walk into a rock wall, and taking slow and careful steps lest he step off a ledge, Antonio made his way forward.

As he did, he saw another pinpoint glow source, and then another…and another. The light was a faint bluish illumination, one he guessed was bioluminescence, but from what, God only knew, and it was an eerie light at that. A spooky glow was better than darkness, though, and Antonio allowed his vision to adjust to it as his gaze probed the spaces ahead.

One foot at a time, he made his way deeper into the subterranean labyrinth, the glow intensifying the deeper he went. He didn't know exactly when it happened, but was aware after a time that he could see without straining, that the entire cavern system was bathed in a low but pervasive cerulean hue.

With this light also came the understanding that this was no mere burrow holed into the dirt by rummaging animals, but a true geological wonder, obviously carved out of the Earth over millennia of patient grinding, drip by drip by drip of water carrying impurities belched from deep within the planet. Stalactites and stalagmites studded the ceiling and floors, glittering with unknown minerals.

Antonio was shocked at the sheer size of this underground system. He pictured the area from above as he had seen it on the way in from his ultralight. The green mountain with its majestic waterfall cascading out of the side, high near the top, falling below into a never-ending explosion of mist. The rain forest canopy had shrouded these wonders that waited in the ground, and now he was experiencing them firsthand.

And what an experience it was. The dripping of water echoed throughout the luminous cavern system as Antonio took his bearings. He found it difficult to entertain thoughts of leaving the cave after seeing its intriguing beauty. He stepped deeper into the underground area, finding that it became gradually lighter the deeper he penetrated. More bioluminescence everywhere, all around him. He knew he should turn back now, though. Looking ahead, there were many branching passages and places to go. Even though it was somehow naturally lit, he could still get lost. The place was incredible, though; he just had to stand and stare at it for a while. Stalagmites taller than he was rose out of the floor, and equally impressive stalactites descended from the ceiling, both even touching in some places to form one continuous column from floor to ceiling. What caused the glowing light? Microbes, he thought, gazing in wonder at the marvelous display around him. Fungus? Maybe some kind of aquatic life form? His thoughts ran rampant with speculation. He had just made up his mind to turn back when his consciousness registered a new sound.

Faint, but repetitive. Different than the water drips that relentlessly fell from the cave ceiling, as they had for countless millennia, sculpting this entire cave one patient drop at a time. Antonio stopped thinking about the cave altogether and focused on the sound.

Footsteps! And not animal, either, by the sound of them, but human. Two feet splashing along. Probably bare feet, Antonio mused. Someone from the tribe was coming to check on him.

The splashy footfalls increased in pace, as if the person was growing more sure of where they were going. His father had said they were guarding a secret here, that they were very protective of it. He had come here to investigate it, and now someone from the tribe was coming.

The steps were very near now, and Antonio knew if he remained standing where he was that the person would see him in a matter of seconds. He flashed on the note from his father (*They are going to kill you*), and moved deeper into the cavern.

CHAPTER 12

Andaman Islands, Indian Ocean

The rain slowed Foster's team considerably. It came without warning, a near-torrential downpour that portended the coming monsoon season. The water from the sky was a double-edged sword, because while it made it harder to track the tribe, it also made his party more difficult to detect. By the time they reached the stone monument, they had lost sight of all of the tribal people.

"Pretty sure they picked up a game trail that way, there." Alfred pointed into the lush jungle, waves of misty steam now rising from the ground as the rain seemed to evaporate soon after it fell. Stel frowned in that direction, then looked up at the falling rain that pelted their safari-style hats.

"Let's set up camp."

Alfred looked confused. "Camp? What for? I thought we were following the—"

"Impossible in this rain. And it's time to check in with the powers that be, give them a little update on our progress."

Alfred threw up his hands and addressed the porters about setting up a camp. Stel ducked under some leaf cover thick enough to provide a semi-dry spot while the tent was being put up. He took out his Iridium satellite phone and placed a call to his liaison at the Indian Office of Indigenous Affairs. After the obligatory holds and transfers, he was finally connected to his contact, a high-ranking administrator with the Office.

"Mr. Patel, it's good I was able to reach you."

"I hope it is, Dr. Foster, I certainly hope so. Tell me, what news do you have for me?"

Stel cleared his throat while he looked back at the progress on the tent; it would be nice to be out of this rain completely. But they were still working on it, the porters stopping to chew some betel leaves. "I'm afraid the news is scant so far, Mr. Patel. The tribal people are extremely hostile and I have been unable to learn very much about them so far, out of fear for my life. As we speak, sir, I am literally cowering in the bushes."

An irritated sigh was audible through the phone. "Dr. Foster, we already knew they were extremely hostile, that's why we retained your services. We're paying you to learn something about them, so that we may be able to solve this problem in a non-violent manner. Also, two Thai fishermen have been reported missing, and although their boat was never found, current and wind patterns would have sent them to the Andamans if they were disabled and adrift. Look for them while you're at it."

"I understand what you've contracted me to do. And while I haven't yet been able to make the kind of headway you expect, nor have I come across any stranded fishermen—I do have a couple of things you may find interesting."

"Interesting?" Patel's voice dripped with skepticism. "Is that interesting as in, oh that's nice, how interesting? Or is it actionable, interesting?"

Stel shrugged to himself in the rain before answering. *These government wankers are the same the world over. Think they can understand things from behind a desk hundreds of miles away...*

"I'll let you make that decision for yourself, Mr. Patel. First of all, these people are speaking a language I've never bloody heard before. You are aware that I am among the foremost indigenous languages experts in the world, if not *the* foremost?"

"Again, Dr. Foster, this was one of the main reasons we hired you. Go on."

"The fact that the language is so unique is highly unusual. It will require further study."

"This is not a research grant, Dr. Foster. We are paying you to ameliorate the situation between this tribe and the passing fishermen, so that clashes do not continue."

"Of course. We did find one other thing."

"Go ahead."

"The tribe appears to be keeping some sort of records in a sealed stone vessel. It's most unusual for such a primitive people."

"And that's all you know about it?"

Stel blushed at the insult. "So far, yes, but—"

"It doesn't sound terribly important to me, Dr. Foster. Remember, you're not on an archaeology expedition here, you're supposed to be figuring out how we can keep the peace. So these artifacts, whatever they are, should only be considered useful insofar as they further that goal. Are we clear?"

Stel said he was.

"Good. You need to make some real progress in order for our retainer with you to be renewed."

"Very well, Mr., Patel. I—"

But he heard the click signifying the call had disconnected. *Bastard.*

"Tent's ready!" Alfred called. Stel turned around to see the rest of his team standing beneath the shelter of the tent. He walked over and joined them beneath the tarp, and not two seconds later, the rain stopped.

"Great, this whole expedition is going just bloody fantastic, isn't it?"

"What's the matter, sir?" Alfred asked.

While the porters unpacked some of their gear, Stel recapped his call with Mr. Patel to Alfred. Near the end of his account, Alfred slowly raised his arm and pointed out of the tent, across the forest. Stel followed his finger and saw a lone tribal man stooping down to collect a bowl or bucket of some sort that had filled with the recent rain water. There were perhaps a dozen such containers lined up, but he carried only one at a time.

"We need to accelerate things on this, Alfred. This isn't going to be as easy as I thought, Without being able to understand them, I can't really act as a mediator, now, can I?"

"I suppose not."

"Not only that, they're hiding some kind of secret with those records. It's just not normal for a people like this to keep archived records on stone. How did they learn to do that? Who are they?"

"Good questions, sir. But how are we going to learn their language sufficiently to communicate in such a short time?"

As they watched, the tribal man returned and picked up another rain water bowl. Stel stroked the stubble on his chin. An idea took shape in Dr. Foster's mind, one that scared and excited him at the same time.

"We need a little one-on-one time with a single tribe member, rather than waltzing in on their terms and having them treat us like the outside curiosities we are. We'll never get anything done that way. "

"So what are you proposing, Stel?"

He watched the tribal man heft another water vessel and turn away to carry it back to wherever he was taking them. "Instead of us going to them, I think we should bring one of them to us."

CHAPTER 13

Brazilian Amazon

Antonio's adrenaline spiked as he reached the edge of a pot-hole like depression in the cave floor. He almost fell into it, a fall that would have made more than enough noise for his pursuer to home in on. He still harbored a faint hope that they didn't know he was in here, that this person in the cave was just checking, just to be sure, that whatever it was they were guarding in here was still safe in the outsider's presence.

But somehow he doubted that. If he'd been seen entering the cave, then that was it. The man behind him was probably a skilled warrior for the tribe, one for whom killing the outsider in their sacred hiding place would be quite the coup.

Antonio eyed the way forward, deeper into the cavern and away from the indigenous man. The bioluminescence was barely sufficient to allow him to move at a decent pace while still being able to see enough to avoid smashing his head into a hanging stalactite, or falling into a watery pit. But move forward he did, and quietly. Never had Antonio been so frightened in the field as this. He'd never met an uncontacted tribe before now, though. *Maybe it wasn't such a good idea coming here by myself*, he thought, as he put a hand on a stalagmite and swung himself around it and over a clump of uneven rock to land on smooth ground.

He stood still and heard the footsteps, approaching faster now. He had to hide. He knew that he had no hopes of eluding this tribal warrior in his own backyard, in his own sacred place he was entrusted by his people to guard. The man would hunt him down and kill him, like an animal. He had seen it done once, many years ago. And he had understood the mistake the man had made, a hunter who had shown no respect for the tribe's territory. He had only to share his meal...Antonio blocked the vicious memory. He needed to concentrate, needed to reason....He thought about simply running until he reached the cave exit, but even if he were to outrun this warrior, once he gave word to the village that he had seen the newcomer there....

Antonio shook his head. To not be seen at all was truly his only option. Anything else would result in his own death, of that he had no doubt. His father's death would be discovered soon, too, and although it wasn't his fault and they would have no reason to think he had actually done it, he knew the kinds of superstitions tribes held. He would be seen as a harbinger of doom, a bringer of bad luck; one minute, everything was fine, the next, this white man is here and one of our people is dead. Antonio wondered what they thought of his father--how he had been accepted by the tribe, but that was something to ruminate over another time. Right now, he had to survive.

He quickly scanned his surroundings. About twenty feet away was a formation of stalagmites, a clump of stony spires that rose from the floor in a roughly circular formation, with what looked like an open space in the center. Probably large enough for him to hide in, if he could slip between the spires.

Antonio heard the footfalls behind him cease. He waited, didn't want to move while his hunter was also stopped, no doubt listening for signs of his quarry. When he heard the hunter start moving again—in the wrong direction, thank God, off to the left—Antonio dashed as quietly as he could to the stalagmite formation.

He reached the formation and circled around it sideways, looking for a space between two of the rocky poles that was wide enough to permit him to pass through. Halfway around, he found it. Antonio heard a loud splash—the hunter's foot travelling at high speed into a shallow depression filled with water---and he slipped between the two stone columns.

He crouched instinctively. He found himself in the center of a four-foot diameter circle of stalagmites. Gazing up at the ceiling, hoping that he might find an avenue of escape in that direction, he was dismayed to see the cavern roof a good forty feet high, with no stalactites hanging down directly overhead. He continued to hear the progress of his hunter as he stood stock still in his circle of stone spires, like a prisoner behind bars. The tribal warrior was in his midst. As he seemed to glide across the cave floor, Antonio saw him in shuttered flashes as he watched through the stalagmites.

There was one last direction in which he hadn't looked, so he glanced down, not expecting to see anything that would change the courses of action available to him. And yet, when he glanced downward, even though he could still hear the hunter approaching, he couldn't tear his gaze from a blackish rock, about the size of a basketball, but cracked in half, sort of like a geode. It cast a similar light to what the natural cave phosphorescence was, and yet as he watched he saw that it changed colors, from blue to green to yellow….orange….

Then, as the glow morphed to red, Antonio saw something embedded inside the rock, something that was obviously a man-made object.

Slowly, Antonio reached down and touched it.

CHAPTER 14

Andaman Islands, Indian Ocean

"Stel, I've worked with you a long time now, but I'll be goddamned if that's not the craziest idea I've ever heard come out of your mouth. Are you feeling okay, Dr. Foster?"

"Shhh, they'll hear us! Take this." Stel handed Alfred a length of rope. "Take it over to that tree, there." He pointed to a nearby *Dipterocarpus* tree. "Wind it around the trunk a few times."

Alfred's gaze followed the rope to its other end. "But this is *insane*, Stel! We're risking our lives!"

Stel dropped his rope and stepped up to his associate. "You don't want to do this? Fine. Go wait on the beach. But when the boat picks us up, I'm going to be boarding with the next tribe member who comes to check on their dinner right here, and he's leaving the island with us." Stel indicated the animal meat cooking on a spit.

Alfred shook his head back and forth rapidly, as if trying to make sense of something that had no rhyme or reason to it. "I didn't say I wouldn't do it, Stel. I just..." He trailed off while watching the meat cook. He brought the binoculars to his eyes and focused in on what was being spit roasted. Stel was still talking, but Alfred wasn't responding. He was just staring through the binoculars, mouth open.

"What is it, Alfred?"

Wordlessly, he passed Stel the optics. Stel focused in on the cooking meat, and then blanched as he realized what he was seeing.

"Is that…?"

"A human being cooked over a fire? I'd say it is, Stel. At first I thought it was a pig, but then I saw legs, arms."

"Not a pig," Stel said, his voice barely above a whisper. "A *long pig*." The term referred to human meat, when consumed by cannibals.

"Bloody fantastic," Alfred said sarcastically.

Stel shrugged from behind the binoculars. "Get out the camera, will you? I'd say we just found one of those lost fishermen."

Alfred took a Nikon SLR camera with a 300 mm zoom lens from his pack and snapped off a series of photographs of the human meat being cooked. That done, he turned to Stel, who still studied the macabre scene through the binoculars. "Too bad his face is completely burned off, no way we can ID him on the spot."

"You still feel like going through with that harebrained scheme of yours, Stel?"

Stel nodded. "This doesn't change anything. Like the charming Mr. Patel said, we already knew these people were violent going into this."

Alfred let loose a long, sarcastic chuckle. "Violent, yeah. Street gangs are violent, but they're not bloody headhunting cannibals. This kind of takes it to another level."

"We have no choice in the matter, Alfred. If we want to advance our careers, then this is the way."

"It's a hell of a thing to do you, you know? You're talking about basically kidnapping a tribal human—one who would literally *eat* us if he could-- and taking him to the big city so we can study him in a lab environment."

"Interview," Stel stressed, "call it an interview for Christ's sake, mate. These people aren't lab rats, they're human beings."

Alfred made a snorting sound. "You better get used to hearing that kind of criticism."

Stel shook his head. "Alfred, we're not going to keep the poor sap indefinitely. We just need to get him into a controlled environment and get him—or her, I suppose, depending on who comes along to check the meal next—talking. Then we'll be able to get a handle on the language. Bring in other outside experts if need be. Then we can actually have a dialog about what's been happening with the fishermen, so we can report back to the lovely Mr. Patel that we know exactly what's going on, and then make a recommendation on how they might proceed, which is what we're being paid to do."

At this, Alfred acquiesced. "I suppose it does make a certain kind of sense, Stel, but come on, even you have to admit it's extreme, so extreme that it smacks of desperation. Why not just admit that we don't know, further study is required?"

"Further study is required, but we're going to take the initiative and complete that study before they even know it needs to be done. Onward and upward!"

"You do realize, my good chap, that if this backfires, it would set both of our careers far, far back—even yours."

Stel leaned in closer to his colleague. "I didn't get to be at the top of my profession by playing it safe. You know this! Years ago I was studying things no one cared about, topics considered frivolous by everyone who was anyone. You remember those days, Alfred—you remember the Asprochaliko dig?"

Alfred nodded slowly. "Fair enough. I just hope—"

"Shhh! Someone's coming!"

Both porters were still back at the camp, which was some distance from the two explorers' current position, so they only needed to worry about concealing themselves. That in itself was a tall order, though, since these tribal people were extremely in tune with their environment and would tend to notice any sound, sight or smell even slightly out of place.

The pair of anthropologists lay prone on the moist ground, watching as a tribal figure, an adult male, approached the roasting human meat on the fire. Stel watched as the man neared the rope trap, which was set low and concealed in the leaves on the forest floor.

The high-pitched drone of an unseen insect was the only sound as the tribal man padded silently across the forest floor toward the spit-roasting meat. Stel reached out and placed a hand on Alfred's shoulder, a warning to stay put, stay calm, until it was time. Stel was holding his breath, afraid of making the barest sound. The tribal person stopped a foot short of the trip rope and turned in their direction. He paused while his gaze was directed that way, but then he turned back toward his food and stepped toward it at a normal walking pace.

Stel yanked on the free end of the rope and pulled it taut. With the other end tied to the tree, the obstruction was suddenly ankle-high in the tribesman's way, and he tripped over it, stumbling to the ground. Stel slapped Alfred on the shoulder: go! The two of them scrambled up into a run toward the fallen man. They dove on top of him just as he was starting to regain his feet.

"Get his hands, Alfred, get the hands—hurry!"

Stel bear-hugged the tribal man, attempting to immobilize him enough for Alfred to hold his hands together long enough to be tied. The sinewy man was a fighter, though, and within ten seconds Stel and Alfred both had blood streaming from their noses, and Alfred a swelling eye.

"It's a death sentence for us now if he gets away," Stel huffed, referencing the fact that the entire tribe would hunt them down if this man were to escape at this point and relay his ordeal. The smell of charred human flesh a few feet away served as an even more powerful reminder of their fate should that happen.

"I've got his wrists," Alfred choked out, his head beneath their target's back.

Stel planted one knee on the indigenous man's side while he pulled the length of rope from his belt that he had prepared for this purpose. With Alfred holding the wrists he was able to wrap the rope around him, even though he flailed. With the wrists tied behind his back, Stel pulled the man off of Alfred and together they pulled him to his feet, with Alfred holding his wrist rope.

The tribal man promptly head-butted Stel in the left eye, which split instantly, sending a trickle of warm blood down his cheek.

"Right, let's get going then, shall we?" Stel said, spinning the captive around and shoving him forward toward their makeshift camp.

#

By the time they reached the camp, the tribal man had settled into a quiet, sullen demeanor, no longer lashing out at his captors. The two Indian porters were shocked at his appearance; he was completely naked, wearing not even a loincloth, and was extensively adorned in tattoos and bone piercings.

Stel instructed the porters to pack up the camp and then he turned to Alfred, who still held onto the tribal man's wrist rope like a leash. "You hold onto him, I'm going to call the boat." Stel picked up a radio and chatted into it while the porters continued to put away the camp. After a couple of minutes, Stel signed off his radio call and addressed Alfred.

"Boat's going to meet us on the far side of the mud flat, where they dropped us off."

Alfred's eyes widened. "The tribe usually has lookouts on the flats. If they see us walking there with him..." He nodded at their prisoner, who made eye contact with them in turn, but said nothing, nor did he try to move.

"That's as close as the boat can get to the island, Alfred. We'll just have to be fast." He looked over at the porters, who were rolling up the tent. "We better get a move on, Alfred. They'll catch up." The porters nodded and Stel, Alfred and the tribal captive set out for the beach.

They entered the narrow game path single file with the captive in the middle, Stel up front and Alfred behind, holding the rope. "Do not let him run off here, Alfred, we'll never find him again, jungle's too thick."

"I've got him, but if you hear me yell, it means I need help."

"Glad we have a secret signal, mate."

"Glad you have a sense of humor even at a time like this. You're going to have to do the machete work, though, my hands are full."

"Fair enough." Stel hacked away at a cluster of thick vines hanging over the footpath, blocking it.

"Why do I feel like a blow dart is going to land in my neck at any second?" Alfred lamented.

"I'm going as fast as I can, old friend. Don't worry, we'll get there."

They continued on toward the beach, eventually rejoining a larger path they had taken earlier. "Ah, this is more like it," Stel said. "We can move a little quicker now if you're up to it?" He turned around to eyeball the tribal man, who looked none the worse for wear, and Alfred, who now had one badly swollen eye, although his bloody nose had been dealt with at the camp.

"I'm sorry, but I'm really not up to it, mate. I'm going as fast as I can already. I don't want to lose control of him," he finished, nodding to the rope he held that bound his captive's wrists.

"It's okay, you're doing fine, just keep moving. We're about halfway there."

They plodded on in silence for a while, more confident now that they recognized their surroundings and knew where they were going. Just before the beach came into view through the trees, the native made his move, perhaps having waited for the trek to be near its end so that his captors would be more tired.

"Will the private plane be lined up when we get to the mainland?" Alfred was saying. "Because I assume they're not going to let us fly back to London commercial with our friend here. Somehow I doubt his papers are in order, not to mention his outfit, or lack thereof, is cause for concern, so—"

The tribesman moved so swiftly that Alfred, concentrating on his next words, was taken completely by surprise. There was a bare foot plowing into his belly, and the rope sliding through his palm, and then the tribal human bolting off the path into the tangled jungle. Only the *oomph* emitted from Alfred's mouth when the native kicked him gave Stel any warning at all. But he spun around as soon as he heard it, saw what was happening and stuck his right foot out, sending him tripping and sprawling headlong onto the rain forest floor.

The two explorers dogpiled on top of him again.

"Don't be too rough on him," Stel cautioned as Alfred started to twist one of the man's arms. "We're going to need to learn from him, Alfred, we don't want him to hate us."

Alfred looked up from binding the man's hands for the second time that day. "What, you don't think kidnapping him from his remote island in the Indian Ocean, pulling him away from his family and his tribe and bringing him on a plane—something he's never even seen before let alone ridden in—to London, is going to make him hate us?"

Stel shrugged while he got off of the man, who only stared expressionless at the dirt. "Look, we're trying to help his people. If we can learn to communicate with him, then maybe we can prevent a full-scale war between his tribe and the Indian government, because that's a war his people will not win. So transporting him is a necessary evil. Let's just go as easy on him as we can in the process."

That said, Stel and Albert pulled the man to his feet, shook their heads at him and said "No," and then resumed their trek along the path. They broke through to the beach without further incident, where Stel scanned the mud flats for signs of the tribe, and for signs of their pickup vessel, the research boat. No sign of either, but by the time they waded across the shallow lagoon—the tide was higher now than when they had crossed earlier—and back to the mud flats, the squat, heavy bow of the research vessel was in sight steaming towards them.

"I still can't believe we're doing this, Stel. I really can't." Alfred stopped near the edge of the mud flat, where it sloped off into deep water.

"Relax, boat's right there, it'll be here in five minutes." But even as he said it, Stel glanced nervously back at the island, hoping against hope that he wouldn't see a horde of angry natives running out of the jungle onto the beach, darkening the sky with volleys of arrows. But there were only the coconut palms swaying gently in the breeze.

"Do you think he can swim well, even with his hands tied behind his back?" Alfred asked, noticing how their captive was staring into the sea.

"Yes. Keep him back from the edge until the boat gets here."

Alfred pulled gently on the rope to see if the man would comply without having to resort to the use of force, and to his surprise he did. Both anthropologists kept their eyes on the beach for signs of approaching tribal members, but the beach remained empty.

During the final minutes of the boat's approach, Stel tried talking to the native, using phrases of other tribal languages and dialects from the Indian Ocean region that he had assumed would be close to what this tribe spoke. None of them appeared to have any effect on the man, who remained mute and showed no recognition.

Then the boat pulled up and a boarding ladder was dropped. Alfred and Stel pointed to the ladder but the indigenous man refused to move.

"I don't think he gets it," Stel said. "I'll go up first, to show him, then maybe he'll go." Stel climbed the ladder and got on the boat, where an astonished crewman drew a pistol and asked if they were all right, knowing the fearsome reputation of Andaman Islands tribes in general.

Stel asked him to put the weapon away and told him the man was coming with them. The crewmen, rather than take this little tidbit at face value, radioed his captain to verify this arrangement. When the captain came back confirming Stel's order, Stel shot the man a smug look and then waved down to Alfred.

"Bring him up, let's go."

Alfred cut the rope binding the tribal captive's wrists, and they all gesticulated to the man to climb the ladder. He looked around once, and for a moment Stel thought he was going to run for it, now that his hands were freed, but then he simply walked to the ladder and scaled it easily. He paused at the top, never having been aboard a modern boat before, and peered inside.

"It's all right, come on aboard," Stel said.

With obvious reluctance, the captive threw a leg over the side of the boat and stepped aboard. Alfred followed close behind, and the crewman radioed the captain that everyone was aboard.

The ship's engines rumbled to life as the captain put them into gear, and the vessel's prow headed across the Andaman Sea for the Indian coastline.

CHAPTER 15

Brazilian Amazon

Antonio felt no heat from the light. Even as it changed to a fiery red, it remained cool to the touch. But *what was this thing?* It was clearly manmade, of that he had no doubt. The light was artificial, not bioluminescence; some kind of LED panel as best he could tell. At first he thought it might be a piece of field equipment left here by some other researcher. But as he passed his hands over the smooth, illuminated face, and his gaze lit once again on the black rock that seemed to encase the entire piece of technology, whatever it was, Antonio could not say with any certainty that this was a piece of research gear.

Whatever it was, besides the light, it also produced a faint humming sound. Antonio placed his ear against the device to make sure it wasn't a trick of the cavern acoustics, but no, with his ear pressed flat against the surface of the thing, he could clearly hear a hum. It sort of reminded him of a computer fan noise. Very strange--what would these people be doing with any kind of technology at all, in the middle of the Amazon jungle, far down in a hidden cave?

Looking more closely at the light panel, there were spots of color that didn't match the overall background, which right now was red. But along the left edge he saw a row of small colored dots: blue, green, black, white, purple....Antonio held his breath as a thought came to him...*buttons?* Was this thing some sort of touch screen panel, like on a ....*computer?*

Antonio wanted to see if he could extricate the device from the rock which held it, but right now the tribal warrior was approaching. Antonio hunkered deep down in the ring of stalagmites, but as the warrior drew near, he knew it was no use. The light from the device between his feet was casting shadows on him, probably making it obvious to the tribal man that something was different about the stalagmite formation.

A sudden war cry erupted from the man's lungs, a high, modulated shriek that paralyzed Antonio with inaction. And then the tip of a spear thrust in between the columns of stone, right past his head to jam into a stalagmite on the other side. A puff of stone dust erupted from where it hit, and then Antonio set himself into motion, knowing he was a dead man if he didn't extricate himself from his fish-in-a-barrel type of position.

The two stalagmites he had slipped through to get in here faced his oncoming foe, so he tried threading a gap on the opposite side. He turned himself sideways and squeezed most of the way through before he hung up, squeezed in place in the tight space. The tribal person, seeing the outsider's predicament, began to circle around the geological formation. Antonio fully exhaled all his breath so as to make his stomach and chest as small as possible, then he tried to move again. He pushed off the ground with his feet while leaning toward the outside of his stone prison.

He fell through the tight columns with a burst of uncontrollable momentum, causing him to fall outside of the circle of stalagmites and onto the rocky cavern floor. Knowing he had no time, Antonio used his momentum to go into a roll, not allowing his body to stop, knowing that his pursuer was only steps away. The move bought him just enough time to bring his arms into a defensible position as the tribal warrior leapt on him, abandoning the use of weapons in favor of hand-to-hand combat.

Antonio had seen the sparring matches many tribes used to train their boys to fight, and he had no desire to grapple with this man any longer than was necessary. He himself was not a trained fighter, and he was under no illusions that he could keep up with a true tribal warrior whose instincts and muscle memory would be honed to a fine art.

He was also clear on the fact that this was not going to be a high school wrestling match, refereed with a winner according to who best performed under established rules. No, unfortunately, the situation was such that there could only be one outcome for this fight, if Antonio was to survive, and that meant the death of the tribal attacker. Any other result—Antonio fleeing to the outside, the warrior subduing but not killing him, or Antonio defeating the warrior but leaving him alive—would mean that the rest of the tribe would know that he had been in their sacred place. That he had touched whatever it was they thought they were guarding—some kind of exotic computer technology embedded in a rock.

He had to kill this man. It was something he'd never done before in his life, never even considered, but now he knew above all else that there was simply no other way for the situation to be resolved.

Antonio grabbed the fighter by his hair—it was not long, but shorn in sort of a bowl cut that was common among many tribes in the region. Still, it was long enough to get a hold on, and he flung the man's head hard to toward the ground, rolling his own body as he did so to add to the momentum. The left side of the tribal man's face slammed into the cave floor, and Antonio knew instantly it was a debilitating blow.

It took Antonio some time himself to recover from the move and to get himself into position to see what he had inflicted, but when he did he was surprised at how easy it had been to cause such terrible damage. The warrior was getting up, very slowly, and when he turned his head, Antonio could see that the cheek bone had been caved in, an unfortunate happenstance of landing on a point of rock instead of perfectly flat ground.

But Antonio had already decided on the stakes, and this was just a big piece of luck toward that end. To let this man live was to sign his own death warrant, yet as he watched the primitive human groggily rise to his feet, no longer an immediate physical threat to him, he found that he couldn't do it, could not bring himself to strike the man again. He stood there a moment, trying to conjure a scenario in which both of them could live…but no such situation would come. His father had said they planned on killing him anyway, even before they knew he had visited the sacred…artifact? Was that what it was? The strange computer seemed like it had been here a long time embedded in that rock, but he couldn't be sure. He was having trouble staying focused now, and the tribal man was upright, coming at him again…

Antonio easily fended the man off with a kick to the mid-section. Even if he did kill him, he thought, when they came to check on the artifact again, the body would be discovered, obviously the victim of a fight, and they would know what happened. The sound of rushing water far on the other side of the cavern caught his attention. This place was close to the waterfall and it was no surprise that there would be an underground river of some sort down here.

The tribal man tried a move on him then, what was supposed to be a feint with his left hand and then a kick with his right leg, but it was executed in such slow motion as to be almost comical, and Antonio easily sidestepped the intended kick. He then moved off in the direction of the rushing water, baiting the man to follow him, because it would be easier if he walked himself rather than having to incapacitate and then carry him.

Even while engaged in this fight to the death, Antonio couldn't keep his mind off the strange device in the center of the cave. It still pulsed deep red, and looking around the cave, Antonio saw that the phosphorescence on the cave walls—at least that's what he had thought it was—now glowed red also. Extremely strange, and he would have to come back to investigate that. But right now he had business to finish up.

Thankfully, the tribal warrior stumbled after Antonio across the cave, muttering an indecipherable chant as he went, reaching out with an arm now and again to make what was no doubt intended to be a threatening swipe, but what actually came out as an uncoordinated, zombie-like flailing. Antonio continued to slow-walk toward the water source, guided by the unearthly red light that seemed to be driven by the strange device encircled by stalagmites. His damaged opponent followed him, unwittingly making his foe's work easier.

When the sound of the water was very loud, Antonio jogged ahead to get the first look at what was up here. He didn't need any more surprises at this point. He turned and ran to the water, leaving the tribal warrior to stagger onward. Antonio felt the spray before he actually saw the water. Cool flecks of mist dotted his face as he walked up to a cut in the rock; it was like a channel or groove in the bedrock through which a fast-moving current of water flowed. He had no idea how deep it was, for looking down into it he saw only black water. The bottom could be just inches below, or untold fathoms, he had no way of knowing and no time to try and find out.

Looking left, he saw that the water jetted directly out of a hole in the rock; no doubt it connected to the waterfall somewhere. To the right, it traversed the cavern floor before disappearing as discreetly as it entered—through a dark hole in the cavern wall, without any kind of precipitous drop that Antonio could see. He jogged across the cave, following the channel of water, which was about three feet wide. Widespread enough for his purposes, but would the exit be tall enough for what he had in mind?

Once he reached it, he could see that it would be cutting it close, but would likely work. He turned to see the tribal man groggily changing course to come at him at his new location. Antonio waited patiently for him. Then, when he began his flail-fighting, Antonio reached out and grabbed the man by his swinging arm, and dragged him by it until he plunged into the swift-moving water.

The tribal attacker uttered no sound as he was carried along the channel. He reached a hand up toward the edge a couple of times, but was not coordinated enough to grasp onto it. When he reached the aperture in the cave, he reached a hand up to try and prevent himself from being dragged in, but he didn't have the strength and was carried away into the darkness.

Antonio didn't know where the outflow of this underground river was, but even if he was found outside somewhere now, at least it might appear that he had slipped, fallen into the water and drowned, rather than being attacked.

Antonio crossed himself, said a silent prayer for the man, and then set about leaving the cave. He'd been down here too long. But first, there was one more thing he wanted to do.

He raced back to the circle of stalagmites and wedged himself inside again. He hadn't noticed the change, but the LED panel embedded in the rock was now glowing green instead of red. Looking up at the rest of the cavern walls, they also glowed a subdued green. Antonio reached down and tried to extricate the device from the rock, but found it wouldn't budge. Maybe he could pick up the entire rock, then? It wasn't that large, perhaps the size of a soccer ball, but would it come loose from the cave floor, or was it attached like a stalagmite? With only one way to find out, Antonio put his hands beneath the black rock and lifted.

He felt the grinding of stone on bedrock, and then the black orb with its embedded technology rose from the cave floor in his hands. He was holding it! Antonio picked it up until he was standing, sure that he was cradling the entire contraption—rock, device and all—eyeing the floor of the cave to make sure no piece of it had been left behind. Satisfied he had all of it, Antonio tucked it into his small backpack (it just barely fit after fussing with the zipper to get it to close all the way). Then he slipped out of the circle of stalagmites once again.

After adjusting his backpack straps for the heavier load, Antonio made his way out of the cavern, retracing his steps, guided by the eerie cave light-- now a deep, cerulean blue. He had a scary moment upon reaching the branching tunnel portion of the underground labyrinth, where he wasn't sure which path to take, but he spotted a familiar pattern of glowing lights and was able to backtrack before getting hopelessly lost.

Slipping into a tunnel he recognized, he followed its slope gradually upward until a curtain of green vegetation was visible, framed against the mouth of the tunnel. He had reached the exit.

Glad to be above ground once more, Antonio set off into the jungle at a trot.

CHAPTER 16

Oxford University, England

Dr. Stel Foster opened the door of an adjoining room and stepped into a small conference room where Alfred and two other anthropology and linguistics colleagues were already seated at a table. Normally, he had many more colleagues than that to choose from, but these were the only two on hand he could trust with such a sensitive matter. Through a window with one-way glass set into the wall, they could look into the adjoining room Stel just came from.

In that room was a similar table and chairs, with two people seated. One of them was a linguistics expert, while the other was the tribal man they had brought from the Andaman Islands. The indigenous person was now wrapped in a blanket—the only thing they could get him to wear—and sat on the very edge of his chair, pushed back from the table so that he was not able to touch it at all. Right now he stared warily at the linguistics expert, who had recently begun speaking to him in various Amazonian tribal dialects, after none of the Indian Ocean region ones had worked.

While he tried to break through to the tribal individual, Stel and the others observed the proceedings from the adjoining room, from which they could hear via speaker.

"He's been reciting phrases to him for hours, Stel." Alfred gestured to the activity through the glass. "Don't you think he would have said something by now if he was going to?"

One of the other linguistics experts nodded. "It does seem unlikely that this is having an effect, Stel. How do we know, for example, that he didn't already say something that was understood, but the subject chose to ignore it? Because he's already through with the Indian languages, he's trying out Amazon dialects, just for the hell of it, but of course we don't expect a hit there."

They watched through the glass for the next fifteen minutes as the tribal man returned the linguistics expert's Amazonian conversation with blank stares. The expert stood from his chair and looked through the mirrored glass, holding up a finger.

"We're going to take a break, Stel, and then I've got one more thing to try. It's a long shot, but it's all I've got."

"Right, let's give the guy a break, have Devin bring him in some water and fruits. So far the fruits are the only thing he'll eat."

While they waited for the session to resume, Alfred stressed the importance that they wrap things up soon. "We can't keep this guy hidden for too much longer, Stel. I'm pulling every string I've ever had just to get us this far, but this is just too explosive—word of this is going to leak, Stel."

The other colleague in the room spoke up. "Agreed. Once the administration finds out that this person has no visa, and that we didn't file any kind of intention to work with human subjects, it'll be a pure scandal with a lot of fallout."

Stel looked sullen for a moment, but quickly recovered. "But it's amazing, isn't it? I mean, you guys are worried about procedures and paperwork, and...look at what we've got here! A living human in the year 2018 who speaks *no known language*. How crazy is that?"

The linguistics colleague shrugged. "It's highly unusual, no doubt about that. But it doesn't give us the right to circumvent established human subjects protocol. After this next round, Stel, we've got to return him to his island."

They peered in on the tribal person, who still sat in his chair, pushed back from the table, staring at the two way glass, appearing to marvel at his own reflection, making faces at himself, shaking his head rapidly back and forth, and gesturing with his arms.

"Of course we're going to return him to his island! I told you the plan was to bring him here *temporarily* for study, specifically to solve the langue problem, ask him a few questions, after which he'll be spirited right back to where he came from. The only snag so far is that none of the languages are a match with his, which is an unanticipated setback. Excuse me for that."

An awkward silence followed, which was broken by the other linguistics expert reentering the adjoining room. He carried with him a laptop computer, which he set up on the table in front of him as he sat across from the tribal subject.

"What have you got?" Stel asked, glad for the interruption in their conversation.

The expert held up a flash drive briefly before inserting it into his computer. "What I've got here are old field recordings of Amazon tribe dialects which are now thought to be extinct. No one uses them anymore that we know of, and no one actually speaks them, although many of the root words are familiar. But let's just see how he reacts, shall we? Here we go…"

The researcher played the audio recording of a tribal elder speaking to a noisy tribal group. The recording was not high quality, especially by modern standards, but the words were legible enough. They all watched the tribal subject's face closely for signs of recognition, but there was no visible change in his demeanor. The linguistics man shook his head.

"I've got one more." He cued up another audio file and let it play, the exotic sounds of an Amazonian tribal chant echoing in the English conference room. Again, the same reaction from the subject. No recognition whatsoever.

Stel slammed a fist on the table in the other room and lay his head on the desk.

"That's it," Alfred said. "We've got to start the return trip process with him, Stel."

Stel felt his hopes of a stunning discovery vanishing before his eyes. Oh well, he thought, there's still that thing Dr. Medina brought up, with that strange language in the little known Amazon tr—

Stel broke off his thoughts and raised his head. He looked at Alfred.

"Before we do that, I have one more thing to try. Have Lelani patch a call through to Dr. Antonio Medina's satellite phone, right away. He's currently on expedition in the Brazilian Amazon."

CHAPTER 17

Brazilian Amazon

Antonio's right foot caught on an exposed tree root and he nearly went tumbling headlong before managing to regain his balance. He'd been running non-stop since exiting the cave, and now neared the point of exhaustion. Fortunately, he had also almost reached his goal. Up ahead, he saw the blue and white of his ultralight peeking through the foliage.

He saw no need to return to the tribal village. His father, after such a stunning revelation, had told him all he needed to know. He had in his possession, in the pack on his back, the very secret the tribe had so painstakingly guarded. It was time to return to his own camp.

He slowed to duck under a profusion of branches, the clearing where he had landed his plane just beyond. His ultralight was there, but a new devious possibility sent a jolt of adrenaline that shocked his system. What if the tribe had sabotaged his plane, tampered with it? He had been gone a long time, now, and if they hadn't started wondering why he wasn't back yet, they would any second now. Hunting pigs didn't take long for these people, they would question it when he didn't come back soon.

He broke through into the clearing and ran to the airplane. A smile took over his features as he assessed its condition: gas tank still there and half full of fuel, tires looking good, wings intact...it had been left alone. To have sufficient takeoff distance, the plane would need to be turned around, though, since he had come in and rough-landed near the very end of the clearing.

As soon as he put his hands on the plane's frame to begin turning it around, he heard the chants of the warriors coming from the game path that led to the village.

They were coming to check on his plane.

*Jesus. Got to turn this thing around....*His hands gripped the support struts and he strained his arm and leg muscles to move the unwieldy machine. After exerting himself to no effect, he saw a rock wedged under one of the wheels where it had come to rest, and he had to take the time to dash over and kick it out of the way. Then he got back into position on the struts and tried again.

The plane began to roll, slowly, but the tribe was much closer now. They made no attempt at stealth as they ran down the game path; he could hear leaves and branches being whipped out of the way. *Come on, come on...*Antonio pushed with everything he had, and finally he had the ultralight turned 180 degrees so that it faced his improvisational runway with what looked like, just barely, enough room to takeoff, if everything went well.

Antonio jumped up into the pilot's seat, cursing as his heavy backpack hit the back of the seat, pushing him forward at a sharp angle that wouldn't allow him to fly the plane. He hadn't had such a heavy load in the pack on the way here. He stood and glanced into the jungle, where he could now see flashes of dark, bare skin as the tribal warriors ran to the edge of the clearing. Then he let the bulk of the pack hang over the back of the seat edge.

He hit the ignition button. There wasn't even enough time to pray that it worked on the first try, he just reached out and did what he knew had to happen if he was going to live through this. The first arrows thudded into the ground around him as the engine whined to life.

*Go go go...*He throttled up faster than he knew was good for the little engine, coaxing everything there was to give out of the system at that very moment.

Images of his father flashed through his mind as the rickety little plane bounced and cavorted down the grassy clearing. The clean-shaven academic, lecturing in a university….the bearded researcher, uncovering new truths about indigenous people…and finally, the tribal human he had himself become, forgoing the society he had been a part of to live like the subjects of his studies...

The plane careened wildly as it hit a rock in the field and for one terrifying second, he thought the left wing tip was going to dig into the ground. It barely cleared, though and righted itself again. He heard the ping of an arrow glancing off the plane's metal structure. He braced himself in the seat, hands clutching the stick, willing it to raise the plane into the air. He knew the archers would be correcting their aim after their near misses.

In addition to the threat of violence from the now hostile tribe, the rain forest itself was now his true enemy as his plane passed the two-thirds mark of his takeoff strip without yet going airborne. Antonio knew that was not a good sign, that if he wasn't in the air by now, he might end up smashing into the trees on the ground at the other end of the clearing, like a head-on car accident going forty miles-per-hour.

More arrows plunked into the ground ahead of his plane—they were overcompensating now, Antonio thought—right before the engine finally caught up with its pilot's instructions and gave a surge of speed, catapulting the plane forward. Recognizing that *this* was the kind of speed the plane need to go aloft, Antonio braced himself in his seat as he felt the plane leave the ground.

Keep going, keep going…he pulled back more on the stick and then used the steering wheel to keep the ultralight level as he aimed for the treetops. He heard the natives shouting over the engine noise. He wondered if they even knew yet that he had their sacred artifact, that it was being carried away into the sky by a technology they couldn't possibly understand yet at the same time appeared to be much less advanced than what was in his backpack.

Antonio yanked back on the stick as much as he dared—too much and he would put the plane into a stall. *Just a little more, that's it…*Another volley of arrows assaulted his plane as the ultralight reached the canopy, most of them missing, but this time one passed through the fabric of the right wing, tearing it, and another ricocheted somewhere off the metal framework. This arrow was deflected such that it hit him in the right shoulder, puncturing it enough to draw blood, but with the force greatly reduced by hitting the plane first.

Antonio ripped it out of his arm with a choice curse and threw it out of the plane as the aircraft's wheels clipped the canopy's uppermost leaves, barely clearing the upper reaches of the rain forest. He willed another ten feet of elevation from the beleaguered aircraft and then leveled the plane out. Satisfied he had done it, had taken off and gone truly airborne, he turned around in his seat and looked back.

The tribal warrior party stood amassed at the end of the clearing, pumping their spears and bows and arrows in a menacing display of anger. Antonio turned back around and let loose a long sigh of relief as he checked his plane's compass. Recalling the heading he needed to reach his team's base camp, the ecologist made the necessary course correction and flew his little plane over the rain forest.

#

After casting a nervous glance at his fuel gauge, which showed the level to be perilously low, Antonio eyed his landing strip and prepared to begin his approach. He picked up his radio and transmitted to base camp. Richards picked up right way.

"Tony, we were getting a little worried, you crazy bastard. Everything okay?"

"Short answer: yes, but we need to pack up and get out of here. This expedition's over."

"Copy that. I hear your whiny stinkpot coming over the trees now. Better concentrate on your flying, we'll meet you on the landing strip."

Antonio guided his ultralight down on the cleared strip, a much better runway than the natural one he had just taken off from. The graduate assistants and Richards ran out to greet him as soon as the plane came to a stop, the propeller still spinning. After handshakes and hugs all the way around, Antonio left with Richards while the assistants tended to the plane.

"Listen, Antonio, you got an urgent call while you were gone—a direct sat-phone call—from none other than our esteemed colleague, Dr. Stel Foster," Richards said as he and Antonio fell into step at a jog toward their camp.

"Oh, good! So he decided to call back."

"Yeah, he wouldn't tell me what was up, said he wanted to talk to you personally, but it sounded important, I mean he was really anxious to—" he was interrupted by a chirpy electronic warbling. "Speak of the devil…" Richards pulled the sat-phone from his pocket and glanced at its display.

"It's him, here." He handed the phone to Antonio, who accepted the call and placed the phone to his ear.

"Dr. Medina speaking."

The voice that came out of the speaker sounded far away, a little tinny, but without a doubt it belonged to the academic rival Antonio had known for so long. "Antonio, I'm really glad I've finally reached you. Thank you for contacting me. You are in the Amazon as we speak, correct?"

Antonio said that he was, and Stel continued. "Listen, Antonio, I know we've had a checkered past, but it seems a rare opportunity has come up for us to help each other." Stel went on to recap his contract work for the Indian government in the Andaman islands, his contact with the little-known tribe there, and their strange, unknown language, as well as some kind of written records they appear to be keeping. Antonio heard the man out, including his account of bringing the tribal man to England, while he and Richards slowed to a walk but continued toward the camp.

"So let me just be clear, Dr. Foster. You're telling me that, even after…*transporting* this tribal native all the way to England for controlled assessment by multiple anthropologists and linguists, that you have *still* been unable to say for sure what dialect he speaks?"

"That's exactly the case, Dr. Medina. Frankly, I'm stunned, I'm stymied. The upshot is that I cannot decipher the language. It's so strange, and in a way it seems vaguely Brazilian tribal. I know you were called in by the Brazilian government to investigate the jungle city deaths. I need to meet with you and see if we can establish a connection between the two tribes. There seems to be a link of some kind, although I know that sounds far-fetched."

"Very interesting. The reason I called you in the first place was to seek your collaboration in formally assessing the unknown tribe I have discovered. Where would you like to meet?" Antonio stopped walking as they reached the opening of their camp's clearing. He needed to make sure he heard this right.

"In London."

"London?" Antonio exclaimed, drawing a curious stare from Richards.

"I know it's ridiculously far away, but that's where we have the subject. It's the only place in the world I could think of to bring him where I'd have sufficient control of the situation. Even so, my own people are clamoring for me to return him to his village, since we have been unable to communicate with him. Obviously, we can't keep him here for long. So you're my last ditch hope, since you're over there now with an uncontacted tribe that, from what little I heard of it, sounded like it had an intriguing language. And of course I'd pay all your expenses, plus a handsome consultant fee for your troubles."

"You don't have to pay me, Dr. Foster. I was the one who called you first, remember? We both need each other. I've got an…artifact of sorts I want you to see, too, that I'll be bringing with me. Let's just leave it at that for now. I'll be there tomorrow, assuming we get out of here before my new friends track me down at our camp here. Speaking of that, I better get going."

"Quite. Very well then, Dr. Medina. I look forward to seeing you on this side of the pond."

They ended the call and Antonio shrugged out of his pack while he looked at Richards. "We're all in danger here. I took something from the unknown tribe and I fear it might be important enough for them to hunt us down."

Richards glanced at Antonio's backpack. "What is it?"

Antonio's eyes widened. "I'll show you once we're in the air. I don't want to take it out right now. Don't ask me to explain this, but I'm afraid it might somehow draw them to us."

CHAPTER 18

The next twenty-four hours were a whirlwind of travel for Antonio, with the means of transportation progressing from modest (hiking through the jungle to the river boat, motoring down various tributaries to the small airport), to modern (landing at Eduardo Gomes International Airport and transferring to a 777 transoceanic direct to London, where he was met by an Uber driver who took him to Oxford).

Antonio straightened out the London Fog trench coat, slacks and dress shirt he bought in the Heathrow duty free shop, figuring that outfit to be much more appropriate than his jungle expedition khakis. As for his luggage, he carried only one piece, a small duffel bag which he was able to carry on the plane so that he never had to let the artifact it contained out of his sight, something he would not be willing to do. He had a scary moment going first through airport security at Gomes International, and then customs at Heathrow. But in both cases, the inspectors never asked to see inside his bag. He was glad, because once, somewhere over the Atlantic, he'd pulled his bag out from its place under the seat in front of him, and, after checking the person in the seat next to him was still sleeping, he'd opened the bag to find the artifact glowing a dull green. He had no idea how to turn it off, if it could be turned off, or even what it was, but private jet travel was not an option to academic researchers unless they wanted to attract a whole lot of audits and suspicion, so he flew commercial and took his chances.

He followed the very careful directions that had been texted to him ahead of time by Dr. Foster, which prevented him from having to attract undue attention to the operation by asking around. It was the end of the business day at Oxford, and while school was still in session and plenty of people were about, it wasn't as crowded as it would have been had he shown up in the morning or mid-day. Antonio found Foster's building without any trouble, pulled open the heavy glass door and stepped into a hallway. He took the elevator to the fourth floor and proceeded down a hallway until he found the room number given to him by Dr. Foster.

Antonio tried the door but it was locked, so he knocked. A British-accented voice called out from within, *who's there,* and Antonio identified himself. The door opened, and he was greeted by Dr. Stel Foster himself. He looked a little thinner than when he'd seen him last time, Antonio thought, but that was a while ago.

"What's it been, Dr. Foster, four, five years?"

"Too long whatever it is, mate. Come on in, won't you?" He stepped aside and glanced nervously out into the hall while Antonio entered, then shut and locked the door.

"I trust the rest of your team made it out of the jungle all right?"

Antonio nodded as he took in the space—an entrance room that was a lab of sorts, or maybe more like a museum back room, with myriad shelves and lab benches stocked with various artifacts: primate skulls, human skulls, maps, globes, stone and bone tools, earthen pottery, as well as various modern tools and equipment such as shovels, ground penetrating radar units, metal detectors and a few Antonio was not familiar with.

"Yes, we managed it okay. The rest of my associates are at my lab in Texas now, with the distinct pleasure of unloading all of our gear."

At this Foster laughed. "Well I'm sure you'll make it up to them somehow, won't you?"

Antonio nodded. "Hopefully with a string of well-received journal articles resulting from the long and fruitful collaboration you and I are about to embark on, are you with me?"

Foster stopped walking and made eye contact. "Now you're speaking my language, chap." He nodded to the bag in Antonio's hand. "Does that contain merely your personal effects, or is it the article from the jungle of which you spoke?"

"It is the article." Antonio hefted the bag. "But first, if you don't mind, I'm dying to see the subject."

Foster nodded. "Of course you are. Let's get right to work, shall we? This way." Foster walked through an inner door into what was obviously his actual office, a medium-sized room lined with bookcases, filing cabinets, and with a large desk bearing a desktop computer with triple monitors. Foster didn't pause here, but continued through the room to another closed door.

"I'm assuming you flew private, but how did you even get him across the campus and up here without anyone seeing, might I ask?"

Foster opened the door, looked inside, then back to Antonio. "We brought him in at three in the morning, wrapped in a blanket, the only thing he would wear."

"And he's been eating, drinking?"

"Water and fruits only, but yes. C'mon in, have a look for yourself."

Antonio followed Dr. Foster into the next room, which was actually one long room partitioned into two smaller ones. A glass window was set into a wall separating the two halves. Even though three men he had never before met were seated at a table in the room in which he now stood, it was the room beyond that held Antonio's attention.

A naked man sat on the edge of an expensive swivel chair, three feet back from the table. The table was covered with food items, including fried chicken, a plate of bacon, some roast beef, but mostly bowls of various fruits. His nose was pierced with bones or small tusks, and his face, chest, arms and legs were decorated with extensive tattoos, mostly bluish in appearance, and drawn in thin, flowing lines. His hair was black, almost shoulder length but unevenly cut. Antonio looked at him and nodded, a greeting he found to be less threatening to tribal natives than a wave or any kind of hand gesture.

"He can't see you through the one-way glass," Stel said. "But before we take you in to get to know him, I'd like you to meet my esteemed colleagues, here." Foster indicated the academics seated at the table and extended a hand to one with a full beard and dressed a bit more casually than the other two. "This is Alfred Algers, anthropologist on the faculty here at Oxford. He was lucky enough to be there with me in the Andamans when I first got the idea to bring this chap home with us." He nodded to the tribal man while Alfred gave a sarcastic laugh.

"Lucky indeed. Pleased to make your acquaintance, Dr. Medina, though I must say I'm far more interested to see what's in that bag of tricks of yours."

Antonio felt the weight of the duffel bag pulling on his shoulder as he reached out to shake Alfred's hand. Before he could reply, Dr. Foster moved on with his introductions, acquainting the two tribal linguistics experts with Antonio. One of them was obviously elderly, and inwardly, Antonio questioned when was the last time he could have been in the field, that is, deep in the Amazon rain forest where these tribes live. He said nothing about it, since he was a guest here, was jet lagged, and because he wasn't a linguist himself at all. The other gentleman, the younger one who Stel said handled the previous "sessions" with the tribal subject, was relatively short on words at the moment, but appeared to be genuinely interested in anything or anyone who could shed light on the mystery at hand.

Stel clapped his hands together, his way of concluding the introductions. "All right then, Dr. Medina, would you care to meet our subject?" Antonio said he was ready, and Stel led him to the door into the subject room. He opened it and waved him inside. "As I'm sure you know, keep your movements slow and predictable, nothing that could be perceived as menacing."

Antonio said he understood and then passed into the room. The indigenous man watched him enter but otherwise made no movement or acknowledgement of his presence. Antonio walked slowly to the table and set his bag on it before taking a chair himself and resting his hands in plain view on the table.

He made eye contact with the man and uttered the two-syllable greeting he had just heard the unknown tribe he visited in the Amazon use when two of their members walked past one another. The reaction was instant and unmistakable. The tribal man's eyes widened while he stared at Antonio. He raised his head and pushed back slightly in his chair.

Immediately the door opened and Stel popped his head through. "Dr. Medina, can you please rejoin us in here for a moment?"

Antonio nodded to the tribal man and slowly got up from his chair and went back into the other room, closing the door behind him.

"How did you do that?"

"What was that?" Both linguists were shouting at him at once while Stel stood and beamed.

"Gentlemen, gentlemen, give him a chance to explain, please! Dr. Medina—may I call you Antonio at this point? Do go ahead."

Antonio took a seat at the table and shrugged. "I'm not sure what the language is called, or if it's even known, but it was a simple greeting I witnessed firsthand only a couple of days ago when I stayed in the tribal village in the Brazilian Amazon." Antonio flashed once again on his father, and pushed the images aside. He hadn't mentioned to anyone, even his own team members, that he had found, and then lost, his Dad. It all seemed too much to convey in addition to everything else that was going on.

"His reaction was so immediate!" the older linguist noted.

Stel shook his head. "But hold on…how is this even possible? How do two tribes on different sides of the planet, both of which may be rightfully classified as 'uncontacted' by modern civilization, speak the same language?"

Both linguists shook their heads. At length, the older one said, "It's unheard of."

Stel turned to Antonio. "Do you know any more vocabulary?"

"A little bit. Let me go back in and try some more things."

The three Oxford men nodded and Antonio returned to the subject room. This time, upon entering, the tribal man uttered the greeting in his native language, which Antonio returned in kind before seating himself at the table once again.

While the jungle native munched on a plantain purchased at a local Whole Foods market, Antonio pulled his duffel bag in front of him on the table and unzipped the bag. He glanced quickly at the artifact, which currently displayed no color. Then Antonio removed the object from the bag—the hemisphere of strange, blackened rock containing the computerized LED panel—and set it on the table in front of the tribal individual.

The subject's reaction was swift and decisive. His eyes widened in what appeared to be a mix of fear and recognition upon seeing the article, and he immediately pushed back on his chair, which tipped over. He sprawled to the floor, his organic plantain flying from his hands. Then he scrambled to his feet and ran to the room's farthest wall, where he cowered in a corner, shrinking to a sitting position on the floor while still staring at the artifact, one arm held out in front of his face as if in self-defense.

The door to the interview room opened and all three Oxford men rushed inside.

"What is it, what's happening?" Stel breathed.

Antonio, still seated at the table, pointed to the artifact, which now glowed a steady but dull red. "This is what I found deep in a cave system near the uncontacted tribe's village in Brazil. They claim to have been guarding it for many generations."

The younger linguist addressed him. "How did they communicate with you enough to get that across?"

Antonio realized his mistake too late, because of course it was his father who had done the explaining for him. Without mentioning him, he was going to have a difficult time indeed of making it clear how he came to know such a thing. With the eyes of three experts now on him, he knew he had to come up with something, even though he did not feel up to revealing what had happened with his father.

"I could tell by the way they placed importance on the cave, how they posted guards around it. They even shot arrows at my ultralight plane just because I flew *over* it. So all that, combined with—"

He was running out of credible things to add and so would be lying if he said he wasn't thankful for the interruption the tribal subject next provided.

In a guttural, angry voice, the indigenous man began yelling at the three men from his position on the floor in the corner, while pointing at the artifact, which still glowed red. Antonio forced himself to block out the sheer spectacle of it all and slow down the man's actual words in his mind. He put his own hands on his temples as he did this, to indicate to the others he was trying to concentrate, before they all started asking questions at once.

At length, when the tribal man paused, Antonio addressed his new colleagues while pointing to the artifact. "I think he's saying that we stole it from his people."

The three Oxford academics exchanged puzzled glances. Stel recovered first. "How is that even remotely possible when this object came from the Amazon and this individual came from an island in the Indian Ocean?"

The tribal man, apparently recognizing that they were talking about him, repeated the same kind of words he had just uttered, with perhaps a touch less anger this time, but he did not lower his hand from his face.

The older linguist held a finger in the air while he commented. "Now that we've got him actually talking, I do recognize a couple of the root words he's using. Very strange, but they do seem to have something in common with the samples of the tribe that Stel played from you over the phone," he finished, looking at Antonio.

Stel focused attention back to the tribal man. "He does seem to be saying that this object was taken from his people. But how on Earth is that possible, unless…"

"Unless they have one, too," Antonio finished for him. "Halfway around the planet and their language appears to be the same. What else is the same?"

This was met with a stony silence, except for the tribal subject, who continued to rant about the glowing object.

Stel turned his gaze to the artifact on the table. "Maybe it's time we took a closer look at this thing you've got here."

CHAPTER 19

Oxford University Computer Science Facility

Antonio stood with Stel in a computer lab across campus. The linguists had been left behind with the tribal subject to continue their attempts at communication, while Stel and Antonio brought the artifact here. They stood next to the director of the lab, computer scientist Dr. James Hanlan, who had a good enough prior working relationship with Stel to be able to promise him discreetness in return for possible publication about the unknown computing device recovered from a cave in the Amazon rain forest. The artifact sat on a workbench with a swing arm magnifying lamp positioned over it. Two white-coated lab technicians were currently bent over the find, working to extract the device itself from its surrounding rock.

At that moment came a knock at the door, and the director moved to get it. "I'll handle this, keep working." He asked who it was through the closed door and then opened it after the muffled response. Two middle-aged men, both bearded with thinning hair, entered the room.

"Stel, Antonio, these are the gentlemen I was telling you about from the Geology Department. They're here to take samples of the rock part of the artifact back to their lab for analysis."

Both geologists nodded, and the one who wore prescription eyeglasses looked at the rock in question. "Hopefully we'll be able to tell you exactly what your device here is embedded in," he said, moving with his colleague to the artifact. One of the geologists carried a small field kit with him, from which he removed a chisel and a small rock hammer. He and his associate donned white latex gloves and then began working with the computer technicians to first carefully separate the main device from the rock. After breaking away the rock at certain key structural points, it came away surprisingly easy, and the technology itself was separated.

"That is some weird looking piece of tech," the geologist who wore glasses remarked as he and his lab partner carefully lifted the geological specimen into a crate.

One of the computer techs laughed in his direction. "Sure is, isn't it? We're gonna have fun figuring out what this thing does." The other computer tech nodded enthusiastically as he gently set the device on the lab bench. Freed of its rock prison, the device looked like a flat screen rectangular LED display attached to a ceramic, bulbous mold of some kind.

The geology pair left with the rock sample, and the two computer techs carried the device itself to a back room of the lab for testing.

#

Half an hour later, after Stel called his own lab to check on the linguists with the tribal subject (they reported he had clammed up again once the object was taken from the room), one of the computer techs walked out of the testing room and addressed his boss. "Dr. Hanlan, after initial testing, we're ready to offer an early characterization of the device."

"Excellent!" Hanlan waved to Stel and Antonio to accompany he and his technician to the testing room. Once there, the other technician pointed to the device, which had been connected by a modern computer cable with adapters to a machine of some sort.

"Let us begin by saying that this device, whatever it is exactly—and we'll get to that in a second—represents very advanced technology. It's clearly a sophisticated implementation…"

Stel cut in. "I don't mean to be rude, but can you just tell us what it does, please? We're extremely pressed for time."

The technician who had been speaking raised his eyebrows and cleared his throat. "Of course. What we seem to have here is some kind of encoded information on hard media, which it seems to achieve using light."

"Possibly even data encoded onto single atoms," the other technician added, "but regardless of the exact mechanism, we're confident that it contains some type of computer code, or programmed instructions, if you will."

"I know what computer code is, thank you," Stel huffed. "But what does it code *for*? What does it *do*?"

"We're pretty sure it runs a simulation of sorts."

"Like a probability model," the technician's cohort added.

Dr. Hanlan nodded to the screen on the machine they had connected to the device. "Can we see it in action?"

"Sure." Both techs said it in unison, and the one closer to their machine pressed a key and pointed to the display. "Watch this."

"I don't see anything." Antonio frowned at the empty black monitor.

"Not yet, but wait for it…there!" The tech operating the machine pointed to the display, where a single dot, a mere pixel point of white, was instantiated in the center of the screen.

"That's it?" Stel asked. Clearly, those in the room who were not computer scientists had yet to be impressed.

"That's definitely not it, the other tech said. "Watch this."

As they continued to stare at the screen, the first dot split into two. "Just like last time," the tech working the machine said. No sooner had he completed his sentence than the two dots had become four.

"Looks like a cellular mitosis demonstration," Antonio put forth. They continued to watch as the pattern of dots, starting small and localized, rapidly grew and spread.

Stel shook his head, an openly critical expression on his face. "A program that does *this* was found guarded by a tribe in the Amazon rain forest? He took a step closer to Antonio. "Dr. Medina, you listen to me: if this is some kind of a hoax, some pathetic cry for attention, I can assure you that—"

Antonio shook his head slowly while making eye contact with Stel. "It's not. I admit that I don't know for sure how it got there in the first place, but my own team are witnesses to the fact that I didn't have it before I made contact with the tribe —documented contact, I might add, since I have video taken from my airplane—but that I did have it afterwards. So if you can't—"

"Gentlemen, please!" Dr. Harlan said, throwing his hands up. "It's not a hoax. The technology is sufficiently novel that we're not entirely sure how it works, but we do believe we have a handle on what it does."

"And what is that?" Stel demanded.

"Our best guess as to what it really *is*," Harlan said, turning back to the screen, "is that it's a simulation of humanity starting tens of thousands of years ago and running through the present. Each dot represents a person. Keep in mind though, that this may only be half of the technology—if there's another half with the Andaman tribe, which seems to be the case according to your tribal subject's reaction. So we don't yet know what that does, or if it's merely a copy of this one. But we've let *this* thing run, and it always stops at around 8 billion dots on the screen, which roughly corresponds to the human population of planet Earth today."

There was a pause while everyone digested this, and then Hanlan finished with, "But it still seems like it's missing something to me, like this is too simple. Not to mention it begs the question, who made the sim and where are they now?"

Stel's face started to redden. "With all due respect, Dr. Hanlan, this is getting ridiculous. What is this circus?" He looked around the group to gauge their reactions, and suddenly Stel's smartphone vibrated in his pocket. He looked at the caller ID and accepted the call.

"Hold on, it's the geologists getting back to me about the rock this thing was encased in…Yeah, Stel here, what have you got?"

He put his phone on speaker mode so that the others could hear the geologist. "So it turns out that this rock you brought back is mighty special indeed. That's because it's a meteorite, as in, it came from space."

"A meteorite?" Stel asked, buying time to process the craziness of it all.

"Correct. To clarify, the same rock would be called 'meteor' if still in outer space, but as soon as it hits the Earth, it, or what's left of it after burning through the atmosphere, becomes a meteorite."

"Okay, okay," Stel prodded, "so go on."

"Right, so all meteorites, including this one, are extremely old. Because of that age, we can conclude that the device you found implanted in this meteorite was placed there not long after its origins, somehow embedded inside the rock at the time of its very formation."

Dr. Hanlan beamed smugly at Stel, who continued irritably into his phone. "But that's impossible, because that would mean…."He looked at Antonio, who also wore an expression of stunned confusion.

"What you're thinking is correct," the geologist on the phone said. "The piece of technology taken out of that rock has to be at least one million years old."

CHAPTER 20

London, England

An hour later, Antonio and Stel were seated at an outdoor table in one of London's better restaurants for a late dinner. Their entrees had already arrived and, after more discussion about the incredible findings back in the lab, talk now turned to what to do next.

"There is only one thing to do," Stel said, waving a forkful of steak at Antonio.

"And that is?" Antonio sipped his glass of mineral water.

"I need to bring our human subject back to his home in the Andaman Islands. He cannot stay here indefinitely, the object was to learn about his people, not to kidnap him. To keep him here any longer is to risk starting an international incident."

"On that we agree, Stel. So when do you leave?"

"Not me," the anthropologist said, wiping his mouth with a linen napkin. "We. I need you to go with me."

"Why?" Antonio set his wine glass back down.

"To find the other half of the rock, with the other half of the light disc. When pieced together, they will tell the whole story."

Antonio flashed on something his father said during his final meeting with him, his father the tribal native. *Antonio, It's starting. I've been expecting you.* Hinting that something had been set in motion, something big and with potentially devastating consequences for humanity as a whole.

He found himself nodding. "All right, Stel. I'm impressed with the work you've done on this so far, and it does seem to lead to the Andaman Islands. I'll go with you to confirm the presence of a second device."

Stel beamed. "Excellent! We can depart tomorrow."

Their server walked up to the table, an attractive blonde who asked if they needed anything. Antonio said he thought a drink was called for, and ordered a glass of wine.

"Great, but I'll need to see your ID."

Antonio laughed, almost blushing, taking it as a compliment.

"Really darling," Stel said, " the man's old enough to be your father."

She shrugged with a smile. "I'm sorry, I know it's an inconvenience, but it's our policy to ask everyone." She lowered her voice into a faux-conspiratorial tone. "We had some trouble recently selling to minors, so management is really cracking down now."

"Not a problem," Antonio said, smiling at the woman. He himself was single, his work and extensive travel routine not having been conducive to marriage. The server left the table and Stel leaned over to have a look at Antonio's driver license.

"Really, let me see, old chap, just how old are you?" He read the birthdate and smiled. "A couple of years younger than me, as I suspected. And I see you just missed being a leap day baby by one day."

Antonio thought back once again to the recent conversation with his father... *What's your birthday, Antonio?*

He was a leap day baby, but his Mom had the hospital put the day after instead of the 29th. But this was more than he felt like sharing with his new friend, Dr. Stel Foster, at the moment.

"Yep, just missed it. Lucky me."

Stel raised his wine in a toast. Antonio picked up his and they clinked glasses.

"To luck," Stel said. "I have a feeling we may need it."

CHAPTER 21

Andaman Islands, Indian Ocean

"I've got to hand it to you, Stel, you really know how to make the most of a research budget!" Antonio looked out the window of the Bell JetRanger helicopter at the silver sea flashing by below. A string of green, mountainous islands was visible up ahead. Antonio sat in the back seat next to the tribal man, who was wrapped in a blanket staring out the opposite window, while Stel sat up front in the co-pilot's seat. The pilot was an Indian woman working for the air charter company Stel contracted to take them from the Indian mainland to the Andamans.

"Wasn't sure I'd be able to swing it, but I had to try. So much faster than by boat, and since we have a limited team and gear, I figured why not? Normally the engine noise is a turnoff because it attracts them to us in a hostile way, but in this case…"

"We want them to find us, because we've got him." He nodded toward the Andaman native.

"Precisely. So Anoushka here is going to drop us off on the mud flat, and then leave right away. Then, when we're ready to be picked up, since we don't know how long we'll be, we'll give her a ring on the sat-phone, right dear?"

The pilot looked over and smiled, giving Stel a thumbs up sign before turning back to her flying. Stel turned back to Antonio. "Just be ready to get out as soon as we touch down."

Five minutes of racing above pristine island beaches, jungles and rocky cliffs later, Stel pointed out the mud flat to the pilot. She corrected course and brought the helo down lower. Antonio scanned the beach for signs of the natives he'd heard so much about by now, but he saw not a single soul. Soon the water beneath them changed to brown sand and mud. The pilot slowed to a hover and then set the aircraft down on one of the drier looking patches of the mudflat. The engine, however, kept running as the pilot waved to Stel while he popped his door open and climbed out of the helicopter.

Concerned about what the native might do once his door was open, they waited for Antonio to get out first, without opening the tribal man's door, so that he would be forced to exit down to the two waiting men. They could not afford to have their ticket to good relations with the tribe run away as soon as they touched down. They needed him to explain what they wanted from the tribe, that as a show of good faith they returned their villager, that they have the other half of an object they have been safeguarding.

The tribal man cowered in his seat once the door was open, shielding his head with his arms. Seeing his native land so close must have spurred him on, however, in addition to Antonio and Stel's waving arms, because he got up and jumped from the door. He landed on the hard-packed mud between Antonio and Stel and stood there, flinching at the helicopter's rotors. Stel gave the pilot a thumbs up and the craft lifted slowly skyward. Once hovering at a safe distance above its departed passengers, the bird headed away from the island, back across the sea.

With the noise of the helicopter sure to attract tribal attention, Antonio and Stel each grabbed the tribal man by an arm, unsure if he would attempt to race off into the jungle now that he knew where he was. He walked along with them in step, though, allowing himself to be led without putting up a fight. They walked across the mud flat, and just before they reached the edge closest to the beach, the tribal greeting party burst out of the jungle and onto the sand.

Five warriors, Antonio counted, all with bows and arrows. As Antonio, Stel and the returned subject stood in place, side by side with their hands in the air, even the native—the warriors began shouting amongst themselves as they recognized one of their own. Then they called out to him, and he called back.

"What's he saying? What was that about?" Antonio hissed.

But before Stel could answer him, one of the archers drew his bow and launched an arrow. It arced high, almost ceremoniously so for what could have been a more direct shot—giving Antonio and Stel time to move to either side out of its path. When they looked back, however, they saw that not only was their subject still there, but that he was now kneeling in place, arms still outstretched to the sky. As if offering himself.

And then a five-foot long wooden arrow tipped with a stone spear point pierced the tribal captive's face with an audible thud. There was a small explosion of blood and then the tip was protruding out the back of his head. He fell over dead on the mud while the war party ran across the beach toward the mud flat, weapons aimed and still shouting.

Antonio looked to Stel. "This is your tribe, Stel, you're the expert here. Plan backfired, now what do we do?"

"Don't move," Stel came back with.

Antonio did, but said, "Why do you think they killed their own tribe member?"

"Looks like we're about to find out. Avoid prolonged eye contact, and don't raise your voice. Let me do the talking unless they address you directly."

"What about the bag?" They both looked a few feet away, to where they had been standing next to the tribal subject. The duffel bag containing the artifact that Antonio had been carrying lay there, a couple of feet from the dead man.

"Don't make a move for it now, they'll think it's a hostile act. Just stay put."

The greeting party was splashing across the shallow lagoon now, in between the beach and the mud flat. Two of them loaded arrows into their bows as soon as they reached the mud flat, while the rest advanced cautiously across the flat to where the two intruders stood with their hands in the air.

Stel turned his head slowly toward the bag and said a couple of words. One of the natives nodded. "Stay here, I'll get the bag," Stel told Antonio.

"Not going anywhere," Antonio confirmed, making very brief eye contact with one of the warriors pointing an arrow in a drawn bow at his heart.

Stel returned at a slow walk with the bag and placed it on the ground between him and the tribe members. He said a word while nodding, then proceeded to slowly unzip the bag. The natives backed up a step at the sound of the zipper, but otherwise remained unchanged. He reached in and removed the artifact and placed it in the packed mud next to the bag so that they could fully see what it was.

The artifact, which had been reassembled into its meteorite, glowed a deep, steady green. The tribe's reaction was instantaneous. All of them knelt in the mud and prostrated themselves in gestures of supplication, bowing down as if the newcomers were gods.

"What's going on?" Antonio asked Stel under his breath.

"They think we have *their* artifact, that we somehow managed to take it without ever being seen by them, which is basically impossible the way the guard it so carefully, so—"

"—so they think we're gods."

"In a nutshell, yes."

"Are you going to be the one to break it to them that we're not?"

"Hopefully their excitement after we tell them that they still have theirs will be enough to spare our lives once they find that out."

"Hopefully?" Antonio gasped

Stel held out two fingers to the tribe and looked at the glowing artifact. He said a word in the tribal language he had just had an intensive course in with the then-living subject at Oxford. The warriors appeared confused, furrowing brows and whispering among each other.

"I told them, this is a different one that looks the same, from a different tribe. But it is the other half of the same whole."

"And they get that?" Antonio asked.

"I think so, but they're going to fact check us, I'm sure, by sending someone to check if their artifact is still in its safekeeping spot." As they watched, one of the men said something to another, who nodded, and then the one who had initiated the conversation turned and ran toward the beach, wading into the lagoon. "And there he goes."

"Wait, wait!" Antonio said, his voice a little too loud. But they all stopped, even the one who had started to run. "Why don't we go with them?" Antonio suggested to Stel. "If their artifact is gone, then they can kill us there, as a sacrifice. If it is in fact there, then they know we're telling the truth about having the other half, or a duplicate, whatever it is."

Stel immediately began translating this as best he could to the tribal men, with Antonio occasionally chiming in. The tribal people then conferred together for a few moments before one of them nodded. That same man then pantomimed wildly while pointing up into the mist-shrouded mountains beyond the jungle, holding up three fingers at the end of his words.

Stel explained to Antonio, "He says they agree to take us on the arduous hike to the place where they keep the article they have, which they still think is the one the we have. If that is the case, as you so prophetically guessed, they will kill us upon arrival to the 'place of the sacred stone'. "

"Why did they kill their own tribe member?" Antonio wanted to know. Stel nodded toward the slain tribal subject and said a few words to the same individual who had just sanctioned the trek to the sacred stone.

"They lament that they had to kill him, but say that he was 'contaminated' by having left the island, and so had to be killed."

Antonio had no reply for this, but he thought to himself that it was all starting to make sense to him. The two halves, his father, the 2-29 birthdays and the two tribes on either side of the world…

The tribal man said a few more words to Antonio and Stel. They need to get going on the trek, which they say is far, three days travel."

"Three days?" Antonio exclaimed. "The Brazilian tribe kept theirs much closer at hand."

Stel shrugged. "Hope you're up for a little hike, my friend."

CHAPTER 22

They set off toward the 'place of the sacred' stone only a few minutes later. Without actually stopping at the village, they passed near enough that other members of the tribe joined the hiking party they heard was leaving to check the artifact, and a couple of those who met the newcomers at the beach stayed behind at the village. Antonio speculated that he and Stel were like new acquaintances you're not sure if you want to bring to your home yet. Stel got a good laugh out of it, but not for long.

"Unfortunately, the fact that they're bringing a hunting party along doesn't make me feel warm and fuzzy inside."

Antonio agreed. The tribe had done their best to explain that the hunting was good up in the mountains where they were going, but since it was far away they didn't usually go there to hunt. "Just taking advantage of an opportunity, I guess. I hope."

"I think you're right," Stel said. "They could have killed us back there on the beach, after all, if they'd really had the mind. What I wonder is, if it's too far to go to hunt, how do they guard it? You would think the guards would hunt before they came back to change shifts, if that's how they do it."

"Maybe they just have guards stationed at key bottleneck points, like the beginning of this trail. Whatever the case, it won't be long before we find out." Antonio picked up his step a little to keep up with the tribe. Even barefoot, they easily outpaced him and his booted feet in their home environment. He started to lower his voice for what he was about to say next, but then realized how silly that was, since the tribe could not possibly understand English.

"There's probably some truth to the hunting thing, but at the same time I bet the 'hunters' are doing double duty as security, too."

They trekked along in silence for a while after that, traversing flat ground that was well shrouded by the tree canopy. Occasionally they forded large streams, sometimes able to walk across fallen logs for all or part of the way, others being able to high-step through the water, and once, even having to swim a short distance. During that swim, Antonio spotted a crocodile near the river bank as he was climbing out, and wondered how much longer it would have been before he was attacked had he stayed in the stream. He knew the rain forest itself is full of dangers even without what he and Stel had embarked upon, but even a small thing like seeing a crocodile really drove that point home.

Not long after swimming the stream, the unlikely trekking party came to the head of a narrow mountain trail, little more than a game path, the opening just barely tunneled out of a veritable wall of thorny brambles interspersed with the occasional palm tree. The path was at an incline almost from its beginning, and at first they had to ford a few smaller streams until it became drier as they moved higher up the mountain. It was still very green and forested at their present elevation, but looking up, Antonio could see how the trees became more stunted, not as towering and majestic, although the canopy cover was still thick.

"I know this must be hard for you, all this walking I mean, without your fancy airplane to carry you over the jungle," Stel teased him as they trudged single file up the steep game trail.

"Yeah, well maybe you should try it sometime. You might find that—"

Suddenly one of the tribe members fired a blow dart into the bush, out of a two-foot long section of bamboo. They heard an animal squeal and then one of the tribe scooted off after it. A couple of minutes later he came back to the trail with a dead, bleeding boar. The tribe indicated it was time to take a break while they cleaned and dressed their kill before moving on. Antonio observed them, thinking of his own failed pig hunt back in Brazil, and marveled at how adept the man was with the stone knife. The boar's meat was collected and its hide folded, cut and actually *worn* by one of the men around his waist in under ten minutes.

The boar meat was shared among the tribe and eaten lightly cooked over a hastily made fire. When offered, Antonio and Stel both refused a particularly undercooked piece, and the tribal men laughed and continued to eat. It occurred to Antonio that both he and Stel could easily be killed here. They were outnumbered, unarmed, unable to communicate effectively, and hundreds of miles from any kind of modern civilization…with cannibals. But he shook off the grim thoughts, telling himself he was too far along to back out now. Besides, he thought, he had to admit that the curiosity over what awaited them at the artifact site made it hard not to want to continue.

Apparently this was motivation for the tribal people, too, because while eating, Antonio caught them sneaking glances at the stone half Antonio carried. He had made the mistake of keeping a spork in an inside pocket of the same backpack compartment, so when it came time to eat he opened the bag and then throughout the meal the tribe snuck surreptitious peeks at the stone. Clearly, the tribe was just as curious as he and Stel were to see if it was in fact stolen, or if it is the other half. And if it is the other half…the other half of what, exactly?

When they were done eating, the tribe indicated it was time to move on. They all got back on the game trail. The stone was heavy enough to be a burden, even in a decent quality backpack. Antonio hadn't noticed it before because he only had to move it a short distance in and out of various vehicles. But now, hoofing it up what was gradually becoming a steeper and steeper hill, with thick leafy plant tendrils slapping him in the face as he walked, it was becoming a burden.

"Stel, I think it's your turn to carry this rock. You take it the rest of the way today, and I'll pick it up in the morning, deal?" Although a small thing, it was the first concrete example of he and his former rival actually working together, and he was grateful when Stel picked up the pack.

"No worries, mate. You wear mine, I pack light."

That settled, they picked their way up the lush mountainside, the air laden with moisture, the sounds of hidden creatures in the jungle around them a constant din. Antonio didn't want to admit it aloud to Stel, but he had developed a nasty blister on his right foot, even though he wore proper socks and boots. He wanted the moleskin he kept in his pack for this purpose, but Stel carried it now because it had the stone, and he didn't feel like asking him to stop just for that, because it would earn him more ribbing about missing his "fancy airplane" and not being up to the task of true jungle trekking. It would have to wait until tonight when they made camp.

The air was noticeably cooler and the sun not visible beneath a blanket of cloud cover by the time they reached what the tribe said would be their campsite for the night. Looking around at the area immediately surrounding the trail, they saw not much more than a slight widening in the trail itself, with thick jungle on either side, as well as being on a steep incline, and wondered why the tribe saw this as a good camp site.

Antonio gestured around at the jungle and uttered the word he believed meant, 'why' in their language. The natives appeared amused, making quizzical faces, one of them even laughing. Then one of the tribe pointed up into the trees, accompanied by a single word.

"There?" Antonio said, the realization slowly dawning on him.

"They sleep in the trees," Stel completed the thought for him.

"Of course. Fantastic!" Antonio's sarcasm didn't stop him from helping the tribe, though, not that it looked like they needed it. Although he and Stel assisted the tribal people by handing them various articles that needed to go aloft with them, it became clear by watching them move about the arboreal shelter that they did not need any assistance. It was the two professional explorers who would be challenged the most by the climb.

Slowly but steadily, they managed by climbing slowly and carefully.

"I'm used to being clipped in when I go up into the canopy," Antonio remarked, and Stel agreed.

"Makes me a bit nervous, too. But when in Rome. Besides, we don't have climbing gear, anyway." Stel perched in the crook of a branch about twenty feet above the ground while he waited for Antonio to select a branch from which to make the next move higher.

"Hey, once we get settled in up there, we might be able to check our phone messages. Sometimes you can get a signal from way up top."

"That's what I like about you, Antonio. You really know how to find the bright spot in the darkest situation. So we can check our work messages while we're sleeping in the trees, is that it?"

"I do what I can."

Above Antonio, the tribal men had completed their ascent, some twenty feet beneath the canopy's uppermost reaches, so that the branches were still stout enough to bear weight. With efficiency that Antonio found impressive, the natives set up a system of ropes, mats and hammocks that allowed them to comfortably lounge about, or even stand and move around a bit. They set up a small cook fire in a bowl on a platform of woven mats they'd unrolled and tied in place, and in what seemed like no time at all to Antonio, the aroma of slow-cooking meat wafted through the canopy.

By the time Antonio and Stel had set up their hammocks (they both had their own modern camping hammocks, since in the jungle it was a gear staple and didn't take up much space or weight), bowls of cooked pork, rice and boiled plantains were passed to them. Washed down with cool stream water collected in their canteens that day, both researchers found the meal highly satisfying.

When it was done and the dishes cleansed with water and put away, the sun was setting on the rain forest. From up here in the trees, they could peek out through the leaves and see a carpet of living jade for literally hundreds of miles. Soon they started to see glowing pinpoints of light flitting about beneath the canopy, filling the space between branches with twinkling amber light.

"Here come the fireflies, right on schedule," Stel said, settling into his hammock.

The rest of the tribe also took up their hammocks, with the exception of those two placed on guard duty—guarding from what, Stel and Antonio speculated but couldn't decide if it was simply jungle predators like big cats and snakes, or some unknown human threat--and it was clear that things were winding down for the night. Like at sea, life in the jungle was generally early to bed and early to rise.

Antonio shifted his weight in his hammock. His legs cradled around his backpack, which contained the stone. He had tied the bag straps to a thick hanging vine to further secure it. He could imagine a scenario in which the pack fell out of his hammock during the night and bounced off every tree branch on the way down to the ground, where the rock and its precious device shattered into a thousand pieces. Not something he wanted to deal with the repercussions of, so he took the extra step to make certain it wouldn't happen. As he shifted the bag between his feet, he saw the red glow coming from inside his pack.

The artifact shimmered faintly in the dark as he drifted off to sleep.

CHAPTER 23

The entire ensemble was on the trail again at daybreak, after a quick but satisfying breakfast of an herbal tea the tribe made, along with more plantains and some kind of "beef jerky," though Antonio was pretty sure it wasn't actually beef. Nervously, Antonio checked his backpack to see if the artifact was still glowing, but if it was, it wasn't noticeable in the early morning light.

As with yesterday, the group trekked in a single-file formation, with Antonio and Stel in the middle of the group, four tribal members ahead of them, and four behind. The four tribe members who were not guards did not walk with weapons at the ready, although they also carried weapons, albeit of lighter "caliber," smaller bows and shorter arrows, shorter, thinner spears or crude yet sharp bone knives.

Antonio found the "militarization" of the tribe disconcerting, and he told Stel so. "They even posted guards all night. How do the ones who stayed up all night get to sleep?"

Stel chuckled. "They tough it out for one day, then tonight, they'll go to sleep early while two different ones will be selected for guard duty. You may notice, though, that they don't put the hunters on guard duty."

Antonio glanced over his shoulder to swat off a bug and look at Stel for a moment while he walked. "That's kind of odd, isn't' it? Guard duty—

wouldn't they want their best fighters on that?"

"That was my first reaction, too, but in reality, they want their hunters in tip-top shape all the time—they are, like you said, the tribe's military might, its muscle power. Anyone can spot a threat and wake everyone up, so they let the hunters sleep."

"Quite a sophisticated operation.'

"Indeed. Not to mention how they guard this 'sacred stone' site that's a three-day hike from their village."

"I've never seen that kind of organized militia type behavior in a tribe— well, except for the most recent Amazon tribe I discovered. They also had a heavier armament than usual."

"And they have a permanent detail at their sacred stone site, correct?"

"That's right. Another similarity between the two tribes."

The group reached an agglomeration of boulders that looked like they came down the side of the mountain in a rockslide, obliterating the skinny game trail. Each member of the hiking party found his own way up, through and over the obstacles, until they resumed their formation on the path on the other side.

"Let me ask you something," Antonio said without looking backwards once they were marching onward and upward again.

"Sure, I've got time to kill."

"I've been thinking more about why they killed their own man back there on the beach, about why they would do that. I know they said—or we *thought* they said, anyway—that he was 'contaminated' by having left the island, and so had to be killed, but I haven't seen this behavior before in tribes. Lots of them leave their village and go into town for weeks at a time on supply runs, it's perfectly acceptable and sometimes even mandated by their communities."

"It's not only that they left, it's that they believe their purpose is to stay here to guard the stone, the sacred stone, and that if they do wander off, they are 'outside their purpose,' is the closest I can translate, and therefore meant to 'terminate.'"

"Terminate…" Antonio became lost in thought as he put one foot in front of the other, allowing the dappled sunlight on the forest floor to lull him into a trance-like state conducive to deep thought. After a while of this Antonio felt as though he was on the verge of a breakthrough, of connecting all the pieces of the strange puzzle he'd been thrown into, when Stel's voice broke his concentration.

"Something else is odd," he said. "This morning, I tried your suggestion of firing up my cellular just to see if I could get a signal, and what do you know, I got one bar, probably from the Indian coast, and so I checked the news I have flagged according to my keywords."

"You're an even earlier riser than me. So what did you find out?"

"I already knew that in Brazil the deaths of those born on 2-29 was a high number, but over here in the Andamans and in India, the nearest mainland, the number was very low."

Antonio almost tripped over a tree root as he processed this. "Wait a minute, you're saying that there were tribal 2-29 deaths besides the Amazon ones?" He turned around and made eye contact with Stel for a moment before turning around again, his forward pace never flagging, to keep up with the tribal people.

"That's correct. I saw, in the Indian online news sites, a back pages article about how two, maybe three people—they weren't sure on the birthdate of one—had suddenly dropped dead in or around the city of New Delhi, with their birthdays reportedly having been confirmed or at least reported as February 29."

Antonio considered this for a few steps before replying with a shrug. "Makes sense, I mean we have both tribes with same language, same birthdates, and now the deaths on the same day—it was the same day, right?"

"Yes, the same exact *time*, even, as near as anyone can tell. I mean, accounting for the time zone difference, it looks like they dropped dead at the exact same moment in time. So yes, they also share the unexplained sudden deaths on the same day, although our tribe here had orders of magnitude fewer deaths than their sister tribe, if you will, in the Amazon."

"That could be because this tribe is so much more isolated. On an island, while the Amazonian tribe has a contagious land tract to connect them to the cities."

"Quite right I expect," Stel agreed.

"And then, of course," Antonio said, adjusting the weight of his pack on his shoulders, "there's the two halves of the same meteor, with a computer program embedded in it, if that's what this turns out to be. Speaking of which…"

Antonio shrugged out of the heavy meteorite pack. "It's your turn to lug this thing for a while."

CHAPTER 24

That night they made camp again only to find out it was another treetop situation. But looking around, Antonio had to admit, there was no where else to shelter, the ground was so uneven, sloping and covered with thick vegetation. But the tribe seemed worried most of all about nocturnal predators of some sort, from which they felt more protected by being in the canopy.

This time, Antonio felt just a touch of chill in the air, being that they were high up on the mountain now. A wispy fog blew across the top of the canopy, reducing visibility, confining their world to a Robinson Crusoe like treehouse existence, of passing things from person to person by tying them to a vine and swinging them across.

And then, after dinner and after the treetop party had settled into their hammocks for the night, Antonio saw it. He actually saw it before he heard it, that's what surprised him the most.

A big cat, a panther, he thought. Black as night. A black panther.

When the fog parted for just a second and the moonlight beamed through the leaves, Antonio spotted the big cat crouched on a Y-fork limb about ten feet over him. He saw the robust paws, could even make out the faint spotted pattern of pure black against lighter black. Then the cat opened its mouth in a silent grimace and Antonio saw the mighty incisors flash white in the moonlight.

He'd seen jaguars in the Amazon, but never a black panther. He was surprised at how large it was, a beefy cat, not a scrawny little thing like some of the leopards he'd seen. This feline was the size of a medium tiger. Something about the eyes bothered him, too. They glowed, but a dull red. At first he thought it was a reflection from the moon, but then it occurred to him that should make the eyes more yellow or silvery, not red....

And then he looked down at the backpack with the stone, and saw it glowing red to the point that it shone through the heavy denier fabric. Glowing the same color as the panther's eyes.

"Hey, Antonio?" Stel's voice whispered from his hammock a few feet away.

"Yeah?" He didn't know if using a louder voice would spook the cat or incite it, but he decided to stay quiet so as not to wake everyone up. So far, anyway, the panther made no threatening moves.

"I see a big cat, over there."

"Me too," Antonio began, but then he cut himself short when he saw the direction in which Stel pointed. Not to his panther, but to yet another one, a few feet above and to the left of Stel. And then, as he turned his gaze around the treetops, he saw many pairs of dully glowing red eyes, dozens of sets of them.

"Why aren't the guards doing anything?" Stel wanted to know.

Antonio looked around and spotted the silhouette of one guard far to their left, on the edge of the treetop camp, perched in the crook of a branch with his bow at the ready. Casting a glance downward, he spotted the second guard in a similar position much closer to the ground.

"They don't look too concerned." Antonio saw that one of the tribal men one hammock over was still awake, and watching their conversation. Wordlessly, Antonio caught his attention by waving and then pointed to the closest panther above their heads, its eyes still glowing red.

In response, the indigenous man nodded slowly, then pointed to the glowing red bag in Antonio's hammock. He then uttered a single word before rolling over in his hammock and going to sleep. Antonio had to rack his brain to recall its meaning; he'd heard it before, during the interrogations in England, but what was the context? And then it hit him, as the fog parted for a moment and the moon shone down on the pride of black cats watching over them.

Protector.

#

Antonio surprised himself by sleeping well throughout the night, awakening only with the clattering of cookware in the pre-dawn light. He propped himself up on an elbow in his hammock and looked around the trees, but all of the panthers had gone.

He sat up and saw that Stel was already up, sipping some of the potent tea the tribe made. "Morning sunshine," he called over from his hammock.

Antonio nodded in return. Neither of them mentioned the panthers. Today was the day they would reach the site of the sacred stone. They still faced another long hike most of the day in order to do it, but it would happen today. *What if the stone isn't there for some reason?* That thought, and the instant death sentence that accompanied the reality it described, wouldn't stop running through his head. The tribe was a simple people, after all, prone to all sorts of superstitions, folklore and thinking that was in general not always based in logic. But he had no choice at this point, he was going along for the ride whether he liked it or not, and so he would just have to hope that the stone was there, as it should be.

And if it was there, then what? Antonio pondered this angle, too, as he brushed branches out of the way and negotiated the steep game trail, which now grew even narrower, ever upward. He voiced these thoughts to Stel, who now walked in front of him, free of the stone pack while it was Antonio's turn to bear that burden.

"Those annoying tech guys said it looked like some sort of computer program simulation," Stel recapped as they marched along.

"The tribe sees it as a god," Antonio said. And then, as a mosquito landed on his cheek, he had an epiphany, a series of thoughts that he was stunned to see accompanied by an intense increase in glow from the rock half carried in the pack on Stel's back in front of him, so that he could see a dim glow even through the bag in full daylight. Green in color. Antonio could feel the mosquito pulling the blood from his face and yet the thoughts were so strong he ignored it, not willing to task his brain with controlling any motion other than walking, so as not to disrupt his synaptic flow.

But then Antonio tripped over a tree root covered in fallen leaves. He lay sprawled on the ground, not yet attempting to get up. The tribe continued walking ahead of them, unaware of what happened, while the hunters behind them had taken it upon themselves to ferret out some small game from a hollow tree trunk.

"You okay?" Stel asked, turning around. Then he saw the strange look on Antonio's face. "What's going on?"

Antonio slowly rose to his feet. "I know this will sound crazy, Stel, but just hear me out, okay?"

"Fine, mate, what's on your mind? Walk while you tell me, though, so we don't attract too much attention." Antonio dusted himself off and started moving again.

"I just thought about this: the meteorite came from space. There's no doubt about that. Lab confirmed. Radio-carbon dating and other tests. So, what if the technology is from not just an advanced civilization somewhere in space—"

Now Stel stopped walking and turned around to face Antonio "Who, hold up. *Space*? Who said anything about space?"

"That's where meteorites come from, Stel."

"I know that, but—"

"They said the computer had to be embedded in that meteorite shortly after it was made, at least a million years ago. This won't stay a secret for long, Stel. You know the computer team photographed and took video of it, so it's going to leak that we have some type of alien technology."

"So you're just looking to find more things for us to worry about, is that it? Because I thought we had enough already, what with the primitive tribe marching us through a remote island rain forest to some sacred site for a possible human sacrifice, that was enough for me...but okay, sure, let's add that to the list, why not?"

"What if the tech is not from space, Stel, but is actually from our human race *in the future*—what if the people who made this computer program are *our ancestors*, and they ran a simulation—a computer model-- a long time ago to see what would happen to their species down the line?" "How would our ancestors have sufficient computing power to do something like that?"

Antonio thought about this for a moment. "Okay, then what if a technologically advanced civilization with unfathomable computing power decided to run models of their own ancestors?"

Stel turned around, still unaware of the glowing green ball he carried on his back. Around them, the forest had gone eerily quiet; no drone of insects, no tittering of birds, no sounds of branches moving caused by small mammals leaping from them. Stel looked puzzled, but intrigued. "You mean, like how certain tech moguls have postulated how we all might really be existing in some computer simulation?"

"Exactly. That we could all merely be software agents in someone's computer model. But don't take my word for it, Stel. Take off your backpack for a second and have a look."

Stel stopped walking, shot Antonio a concerned glance, and removed the pack. His eyes bugged out when he saw the intense green glow coming from within. He put a hand on the outside of the pack. "It's not hot. Jesus, Antonio, when did it start doing that?"

"As soon as I had that thought, about the computer simulation of our ancestors."

Stel's mouth dropped open and he remained speechless, shaking his head back and forth. "What on Earth..."

It was Antonio's turn to shake his head. "Not on *Earth*, Stel. What in the *universe?*"

"How can it read your thoughts like that? How does it manifest things in real life? I don't understand!"

"I don't either, yet, but here's another example of manifesting things in real life, Antonio: Thinking about the 2-29 deaths, the ones who died right away—they all had the leap day birthday, right? So do you remember the Y2K scare? The fear that computers would crash in the year 2000 because of a leap day rollover glitch?"

"Yes, turned out to be a whole lot of nothing."

"It turned out to be nothing because systems were prepared for it ahead of time. My point is, what if that's what this is? The two tribes were entrusted with the original program—they were closest to the source of the simulation app, meaning they were the first humans created with the program—that's why they're such primitive, uncontacted tribes—but, when some of them –centuries later—left the tribal areas for the cities, on that certain day, the program terminated them as some kind of exception error."

Stel looked down at the still-glowing pack. "Exception error?"

Up ahead, they heard the natives calling back to them. "We better get moving."

CHAPTER 25

As they neared the top of the mountain, Antonio knew they had to be getting close to their destination. The jungle did, too, it seemed. Around them, the presence of predators increased steadily as they neared the apex. There was an absence of the black panthers from the previous night, but there were other big cats—leopards, even a large tiger that stalked just out of sight along the game trail, brief glimpses of its orange and black hide the only evidence of its presence.

It was not a cat, but an ape that attacked them first. A stout mountain gorilla, one that ran onto the path from the side, crashing into the tribesmen up ahead of Antonio and Stel. The hunters battled it down with spears and arrows, and after a short but brutal fight, the primate skulked off into the bush, dragging a broken spear sticking out of its left leg.

No sooner had they recovered from that and resumed their upward progress on the now barely visible trail, than a massive python dropped on Stel and Antonio from the trees. It began coiling itself around Stel's entire upper body, its impressive musculature rippling with the effort. The hunters behind them proceed to eviscerate the animal with their bone knives, eating some of the meat raw before casting the rest aside.

"The panthers were protecting us last night, and they were strange," Antonio observed, "while these animals seem normal but they are attacking us."

"Maybe it's normal?" Stel threw out. "It's not like either of us have ever been here before. In fact, I'd say this is by far the most remote location on Earth that I've ever been to. We haven't even spotted an aircraft in I don't know how many days."

"Most remote place I've ever been, too. But I'm an ecologist, Stel, remember? And I can tell you that it is anything but normal for these keystone predators to be acting in this way." He batted a biting insect the size of his outstretched hand away from his throat.

"I wonder," Stel said, "has the tribes' sacred rock always been where it is, up here, or is this where they took it to keep it safe?"

"You mean, did they find it here or find it somewhere else and take it here?"

"Right."

"Good question, let's try to ask them." They reached a small stream whose damp bank paralleled the game trail. Antonio called out to the hunters behind him, but before he could get a definitive answer, they reached a small hole in a wall of wet rock into which the stream disappeared. Antonio shivered involuntarily as he flashed on the tribal man he had banished into a similar stream in the Amazon cave.

The entire group gathered outside the hole in the rock. One of the tribal men looked at Stel and Antonio and then pointed into the opening, accompanied by a grunted word.

"What'd he say?" Antonio asked.

Stel took a deep breath. "We go." Then he shrugged off the pack and handed it to Antonio. "And here, your turn to lug our favorite souvenir."

Antonio stared at the meteorite, which currently was not glowing at all. Then he picked it up and put on the backpack.

"What about light, won't it be dark in there?" Antonio voiced his concern as he peered into the opening in the mountain's peak. He shrugged off his backpack and hunted around inside it for a flashlight, but the tribesmen acted unconcerned. They ducked the cave lip as they waded in the middle of the stream into the mountain's rocky insides. One of the hunters waited outside until Antonio and Stel entered the opening. Only then, with a last look around outside through the notch of a drawn bow, did the tribal hunter enter the cave.

The entire party now inside, they ventured a short distance in the wet stream bed itself, where they still had some natural light. Antonio was concerned because he didn't have his flashlight, but inside, the walls of the cave glowed with the same kind of strange phosphorescence he'd seen in Brazil, giving off sufficient light to see by. He found it hard to believe the uncharacteristic illumination could be a coincidence.

The stream bed sloped downward as they worked their way deeper into the bowels of the mountain. As they neared the artifact, moving down a slick slope, the half-rock glowed insanely, sort of a purple shade. Everyone was talking, shouting, as they neared a pit, at the bottom of which was situated the source of a cerulean blue glow.

Antonio was having doubts about being here. He told Stel, who hadn't said anything back to him in a little while, "I've been thinking about what's down there, Stel, and you should know that means that, because of the code, because of the particular way it's coded, you know—that I won't—I can't--I literally cannot—go any further or…"

Antonio stopped in place, the tribe all rushing past him, Stel urging him on, but waiting for now. "C'mon, Antonio, we're almost there, let's see what it is!"

The ecologist shook his head. "I can't, I'll die!"

What are you talking about, they all want to go, look at them!" Indeed, the tribe members were egging them both on enthusiastically, seeing the wildly glowing half-rock they carried, but no longer afraid of it now that they saw the one they were entrusted with was still there. But Antonio shook his head firmly.

"If I get too close to it, I'll be a another damn boundary error! Like the indigenous people who died all at once. I'll cease to exist BECAUSE I'VE BEEN DELETED, STEL—TERMINATED AS A RESULT OF A PROGRAMMING INSTRUCTION THAT TREATS MY CIRCUMSTANCE AS A FATAL RUNTIME ERROR, DON'T YOU

GET IT YET! We're not 100% human, Stel. We're software entities, all of us, created by lines of code that tell us how to behave, code that determines whether we live or die depending on our circumstances. That's what these machines are, Stel. They're the devices that control the simulation that *is* humanity. I beg you to reconsider our actions here. We've seen enough."

Stel shook his head rapidly back and forth many times. "Sorry, pal, but I don't think you have much choice."

As Antonio looked around, a cluster of tribe members encircled him, all aiming weapons his way. They had no idea what he had actually said, but his reticence and general lack of willingness to move forward was apparent.

"Here, I'll give you the stone!" Antonio started to take off his pack, which burst through with radiant light of rapidly shifting colors, when a short arrow pierced the dirt ground between his feet.

Stel nodded toward the pit, where the same light show emanated from the bottom. "Tribe says we all go."

Reluctantly, Antonio cinched his backpack in place again. They reached the edge of the pit and begin climbing down a series of precarious handholds. The tribe members began the descent first. One tribal man was unable to concentrate, looking down too much at the light, and he fell to his death, landing hard below, silent thereafter. The luminosity at the bottom of the pit increased.

The rest of them continued their descent, some of the tribe seeming to go mad with delirium, whooping and hollering and yelling. As they neared the bottom, it was plain to see that the other half-stone was there. The other half of the meteorite, of the simulation, Antonio thought. His movements were slow and deliberate as he thought not only about which hand- and foot-holds to use, but about the larger scenario now unfolding in all too real-time.

Stel called out, "I see it! It's there, Antonio, do you see it?"

But when he received no answer he swiveled his head to look over at Antonio, and the ecologist disappeared before his very eyes, vanishing in a wispy diffusion of light.

CHAPTER 26

Antonio stood in a tranquil forest with a grassy floor. His father was there also, standing by his side as they prepared to go for a day hike in their local woods. A glowing red border framed the entire scene, but neither commented on it, as if it was a given that it was there.

"Let's go for a walk," his father said. "There's something I need to show you." His Dad was younger, as he was in his working prime and not as Antonio saw him with the tribe in the Amazon jungle. Antonio, though, was still his current age, like a weird dream where things were mixed up and couldn't really happen, but that's how it was.

"Where are we going?" Antonio asked, but his father only waved him along in a friendly way, clearly excited to show him whatever it was.

"Not far. There's something in this place, our place that you know so well, that will help you to understand things better." He added nothing further, so Antonio walked along with him, stopping now and then to point out a fox peeking out from its den or a hawk circling high above, watching all in the domain.

They crossed over a gurgling brook into a clearing of lush green grass with strange plants bearing exotic flowers here and there. Odd insects abounded, too, creatures that at first glance seemed familiar, like a butterfly or a dragonfly, but on closer inspection revealed that they had eighteen legs, for example, or four wings, in the case of the butterfly, or no eyes, in the case of the dragonfly. Just not quite right.

Then his father pulled out a handheld electronic device of some sort, probably a smartphone, but as in a dream, something was off about it, too, as his hand seemed to pass all the way through it when he tapped the glass.

"I have a puzzle I want you to solve. It has a single, definitive answer. No tricks. Once I press this button, you will have until exactly…" He paused while he looked at the clock on his device. "…Four O'clock."

"What time is it now?"

"3:48. It's not a lot of time, but it's all you need if you think clearly."

"Okay." Antonio had no idea why that made him feel okay. It sure didn't seem like a lot of time to solve an unknown enigma, but then again, he didn't know what the puzzle was yet.

"And…begin." Diego Medina pecked his finger on his device's screen, causing it to ripple and move as if it was the surface of a pond, and then a series of shapes materialized in the clearing around them.

"Shapes" was the best that Antonio's flabbergasted mind could come up with at the moment, but they weren't mere shapes. They were objects, by the looks of it, real things that had somehow been instantiated right before his very eyes, and very realistic looking. Antonio thought they were 'realistic looking' and not actually real, since how could something real magically materialize out of thin air? They must be holograms, he thought. But unlike the holograms he'd seen before, these seemed impossibly dense.

He walked over to the nearest one of them, a large hedge that was carefully manicured and trimmed. He put a hand out into the hedge, expecting it to pass through an illusion of light. He caught his breath when he felt the prickly sensation of small leaves brushing against the skin of his right hand. Antonio turned around to ask his father about how this was possible, but his Dad had disappeared from sight.

"Time is ticking, Antonio. Good luck." He heard his voice issuing from thin air but, looking all around, could not see him. What the heck, he thought, it's only a few minutes. He decided to focus on the puzzle.

Turning back to the scene in front of him, Antonio was pleased to see a vivid depiction of what could only be described as the Garden of Eden. A scene of nature in its perfect, unspoiled state. Antonio walked into a pristine forest, even more so than the rain forests he studied, yet at the same time it was far less frightening. Animals moved about their natural business, sloths lounging in trees and wild horses running through the grass. As an ecologist, of course, the myth of Eden as a flawless, pristine Earth before humans came along and ruined it all appealed to Antonio.

And then he saw the man. Naked as the day he was born, or created, as the case may be, standing on a smooth round rock, surrounded by large, colorful butterflies. He didn't recognize him, but he knew who he was all the same.

Adam. Of course, no Garden of Eden setting would be complete without Adam and....Antonio looked around but didn't see an Eve. But as he watched the man, Adam stuck his hand into his own side, piercing the flesh, blood raining down his side and thigh, horrifying ripping sounds reaching Antonio's ears.

"Stop, what are you doing?" Antonio yelled, but Adam didn't hear him. His face showed visible strain as he reached inside his own body and cracked one of his own ribs off with an audible, atrocious *snap*. Then he pulled the bone out, held it up in the air, and lightly tossed it onto the grass beneath a flowering tree.

It began to rain, a hard, warm, cleansing rain that washed away Adam's blood and healed his wound. It stopped a few seconds later and standing there beneath the tree was a beautiful woman, naked but for a strategically placed fig leaf.

Eve.

Antonio grinned as he watched her look at Adam and smile coyly. *Well this could get interesting,* he thought in a male-driven kind of way, but then he caught movement in the tree above Eve's head and looked in time to see a snake winding its way down a branch that drooped beneath its weight. It wasn't a slender snake, either, but a fat, bulging python like the one Antonio had seen in the Andamans. As the snake moved across the branch it dislodged an apple, which fell to the grass at Eve's feet. She picked it up, turned it over in her hand for a moment while Antonio shouted, "No!" But of course she didn't hear him.

She put her lips on the skin of the forbidden fruit and sunk her teeth into it. It seemed to Antonio that he had extra-sharp vision as he watched the juice from the apple run down the remaining unbroken skin and drip through the air to land on the blades of grass below, like sticky dew drops.

When Antonio lifted his gaze from the grass to the wider scene, he saw Adam dissolve in front of his eyes into a skeleton. Not just a skeleton, either, but a processed, clean skeleton, hanging from a stand...in a classroom, a perfect human anatomy teaching aid except for the fact that it was missing one rib. Antonio felt dizzy for a moment as he realized he knew the scene.

His high school classroom, with Mr. Verger's AP Biology class from his senior year, if he wasn't mistaken. "Settle down, people" Verger was saying. "Don't forget that tomorrow is our field trip to the zoo..."

And just like that, the entire scene around Antonio seemed to swirl and dissolve yet again into chaotic light and then re-solidify into...

The front gate of a small city zoo. Antonio was alone, but he walked inside, looking at the exhibits. He stopped at the largest one, featuring a huge moat around a lavishly landscaped enclosure, in the center of which, on a pedestal in a simple cage, was a rat.

Ridiculous, Antonio thought. What kind of zoo goes through all this trouble to display a common rat? He moved on to the next exhibit, which was an ox in an unadorned wooden stall. Antonio shook his head at the awful living conditions for the beast in what was supposed to be a zoological garden, and again continued on. The zoo frustrated him, for all of the animals were seemingly ordinary and not very exotic at all. A regular pink pig. A common rabbit. A black garter snake, a mongrel dog. The one animal which truly held any interest for him at all was a Komodo Dragon, five feet in length and flicking its black, forked tongue at Antonio while watching him with its unreadable black lizard eyes.

That's it, I'm out of here. Where's the exit? He looked around but couldn't see one, confused at how he could have gotten lost in such a small zoo.

Then he saw movement and spotted a brown and green rooster running loose on the path ahead of him. He followed after it and it cut to the right. He broke into a jog to keep up with the bird as it zigged and zagged through the zoo, until it ran out onto a busy city street.

Antonio thought it would be crushed under the wheel of a city bus but the bird seemed to vanish beneath the wheel rather than be actually crushed, and after the bus passed by Antonio saw the rooster running up onto the sidewalk, fluffing its wings as if annoyed. He dashed across the street after it and the bird skedaddled into a casino, of all places, bright neon and LED screens on the outside advertising best games, loosest slots, coldest drinks, 24/7!

Antonio entered the establishment and passed by a few game tables, including one with a full deck of cards spread out, in order--kings, queens and jacks staring up at him as he strode by--their eyes actually moving to follow him. He stopped at a craps table, where a gorgeous woman in a tuxedo worked as dealer. It took a moment for Antonio to recognize her as Eve from the garden of Eden. The same woman.

"Hey—" he started to say, but she was all business, cutting him off to begin explaining the rules of the game as she handed him the dice. "Your roll." She smiled tantalizingly. Antonio rolled: double sixes. Her face took on a mock frown as she scooped up his money.

"I'm sorry, you're not a winner. Would you like to try again?"

Antonio didn't know why he felt such anger, but he was suddenly boiling over inside. "Hey, that's not fair, you cheated! You're not a good person, you ate the apple! You—" But then a large, male bouncer showed up and grabbed Antonio forcefully by the upper arm. He dragged him away from the craps table to the entrance and tossed him out onto the street…

But the scene outside was no longer a city, but once again a grassy, garden-like area. He was standing in front of a carefully pruned hedge, a large one that was head high and seemed to run on in both directions for quite a ways. He couldn't see over it so he began walking around it, noting that it had a lot of sides. By the time he got back to the casino entrance, where the bouncer now blocked the door with his arms crossed, shaking his head at Antonio, he had counted twelve sides to the hedge, a shape Antonio knew from geometry class to be a dodecahedron. He had no idea why he was thinking these strange thoughts, but after looking at the hedge again, he saw it had an opening just large enough for a person to pass through, and that inside, corridors of green wound this way and that.

A maze.

Antonio entered and began winding his way through, sometimes reaching a dead end and retracing his steps, but continuing toward the center of the living labyrinth. At one dead end he saw a calendar hanging on the wall. Completely out of place, sure, but nothing seemed too strange in this odd arena, so he stepped up to it and took a look.

A picture calendar, the kind of custom printed product one could order online if they submit whatever photos they want used, one for each month. Antonio began to flip through it…January was a picture of his family standing in the snowy yard of their house when he was a boy, his parents both smiling, a snowman next to Antonio. He flipped the page and looked at February: a photo Antonio himself had taken of his father handing his mother a bouquet of red roses while kissing her on the cheek. February, Valentine's Day. But there was something else special about February…he looked down at the bottom of the month, but it ended on the 28th day, it was not a leap year, hence his true birthday was not represented.

Antonio left the calendar and pursued the maze again. He wound his way to the center, which was a small open area with a table in the middle of it. On the table was placed a chunk of silver rock. Antonio went to it and picked it up. Not actually silver, but magnesium, he thought, hefting the specimen in his hand, which was lighter than expected for how large it was. He shrugged and threw the rock into the bushes, then climbed up onto the table to get a look over the hedge.

In the distance he could see a flag waving at the top of a pole. It was blue with a circle of yellow stars. He wasn't sure what flag that represented, so he decided to take a closer look, because maybe it could tell him where he was? He got down from the table and started to exit the center of the maze to retrace his steps to the exit, when he decided to try something. He walked into the wall of hedge facing the flag, and found he could simply pass right through it as though it wasn't there. He emerged in a grassy field with clear open space all the way to the flag.

He reached the flagpole and stared up at the flag fluttering in a zephyr. Still only blue with a circle of yellow stars. *But I've seen that before...it's the flag of the European Union?* Strange, he thought, he couldn't possibly be in Europe now, but nothing else seemed to be ordinary about this dreamland, so he didn't think much of it. Feeling drawn to the flag, he walked to the pole and pulled on the rope, attempting to lower the flag, but although he pulled, the flag never got any closer.

Suddenly a decorated tribal man, thin sticks protruding from his nose in all directions like porcupine quills, emerged from a topiary animal, a hedge carefully manicured to resemble a larger-than-life wild boar.

The man spoke to him. "Do you want some gold?" he asked in fluent English. "Have some gold, it is only fair you get your share! Your people have stolen it from our jungle for centuries! Look, we will even weigh it out for you so you can see that you're getting your fair share!"

The man extended an arm toward a hefty gold nugget on a scale. Antonio moved to the gold, but when he picked it up the tribal man laughed as the scale needle slammed to zero and kept spinning around and around counterclockwise even though that made no sense, and then the dial of the analog scale transitioned to a digital scale, its display reading 0.00000000000, before morphing into a video screen, playing a movie...

Antonio watched the screen as his father prepared his ultralight plane for flight. He was in the rain forest, and a timestamp in the lower left corner of the video confirmed what Antonio already suspected with a knot of trepidation in his stomach: 06/12/97, the day his father "died."

He was watching a video of him preparing to take off on his fateful flight, the one that took him—purposefully—away from his life as he knew it, his job, his friends, his family...

Diego Medina cursed under his breath as he tried to get the battery to start. The motor coughed and sputtered with each crank but wouldn't hold. This was heartbreaking for Antonio to watch, because if only that motor hadn't started that day…

"C'mon you old piece of…" his Dad barked on screen. "Give me those volts!"

The motor fired to life and his Dad grinned as the picture—the entire video apparatus--disintegrated into a loose pile of Amazon canopy leaves fluttering to the ground at Antonio's feet.

And then his father was standing here in front of him, holding his strange phone thing in his hand.

"What's the answer, Antonio?"

The puzzle was bizarre; he wasn't sure what he was supposed to do. All of these objects, or scenes he had witnessed, they must have something in common, but what was it? Some of them were directly connected to his personal life, like his classroom and the calendar, while others, such as the casino, were not. But even so, they must have something that unites them at some core part of their identity, Antonio thought. But what?

"You have only thirty seconds remaining, Antonio."

Thirty seconds!

He flashed on the scenes he had been a part of here, and what they had in common. The calendar—twelve months, the roses—a dozen roses—the magnesium—atomic number 12. There were others where he wasn't sure of the significance, *like the flag….wait a minute, the stars*—he hadn't counted them but he guessed now that there would be twelve stars. What about the zoo animals, though, what was the connection there? The seemingly ordinary animals: rat, rooster, ox, but there was a dragon, too…And then it hit him. The signs of the Chinese zodiac--twelve of them! The craps game: he'd rolled double sixes (twelve). The deck of cards on the table showing the twelve suit cards. What about the Eden scene though, where was the twelve there? Then he pictured Adam's naked skeleton, hanging in his high school—his twelfth grade—classroom, the rib cage missing a single rib, but there should be…*twelve* ribs per side. The dodecahedron maze. The gold on the scale—weighing exactly one pound—but not really one pound, because precious metals are weighted in *troy*, so one troy pound, which is made of exactly twelve troy ounces. And the last piece, the video of his Dad starting his ultralight? His mind's eye alighted on his father cursing at the battery as it struggled to start the machine, the *12 volt* battery.

There it was. It was the only thing he could think of that was there in every piece of the puzzle, and there had been, in fact, twelve different scenes, or pieces of the puzzle itself, Antonio realized. All of those seemed to have that number at some core part of their...of what made them *them*, Antonio thought.

"I know what it is, Dad."

"Your answer, son?"

"Twelve."

His father beamed and tapped on his device some more. "Congratulations, Antonio. All those things, they all had the number twelve in common, right?"

"Right, Dad. I got that."

"But do you know what else has the number twelve in common, Antonio? *You* do. Because your real age, in leap years, is twelve. You're *twelve* years old, Antonio. You've had twelve real birthdays in your lifetime, even though people think of you as being 48. You've got to keep those two things separate you know, it's very important."

"What two things?""

"Your real age and the common, uninformed age everyone thinks you are. Those are two things you've got to keep separate. I repeat, Antonio..."

His Dad leaned in close. "You've GOT TO KEEP THEM SEPARATE. KEEP THEM APART FROM ONE ANOTHER, ALWAYS KEEP THEM FAR APART!" His father was angry now, yelling at him.

"Okay, Dad, all right! I'll keep them apart, I promise, I'll keep them apart..."

CHAPTER 27

The game dissolved in a cloud of pixelated vapor and Antonio was back in the Andaman Islands, in the cave, at the bottom of the pit next to Stel, and the dead tribal man who'd fallen, along with the rest of the tribal party who had made it down safely in one piece. Stel had the half-rock that Antonio had left behind when he disappeared, and was about to put it on top of its other half. Both glowed red fiercely.

"No, wait!" Antonio shouted. "Keep them apart!"

"What?" Stel looked at him like he was crazy.

"Don't let them touch! Keep the two halves apart! *Keep them apart!*"

"How did you get back here? Where did you go?"

"No time to explain, Stel. Just give me the meteorite, please! Don't let them touch!"

"Why not, they're obviously two halves of the same whole."

"No, they were made to stay apart, far apart! If they come together, we die, Stel. Not just us, either, but all of us--the simulation program will be deleted and the entire human population on this planet will *reset to zero.*"

"What are you talking about? How can you possibly know this?"

"Joining the two halves will initiate a self-destruct routine that shuts down the simulation, Stel! That's why the two tribes live so far apart, why they were entrusted with the two halves, because they would never come into contact with each other, they were to remain *uncontacted* from not only each other but the rest of the planet as well, for as long as possible, so that no one would ever put the two halves together and destroy our simulation."

Around them the tribal men began to get hot and feel itchy, uncomfortable, not right. Antonio showed them how when the pieces are pulled further away, the symptoms abated. When brought back closer together again, they returned. "If we put them all the way together," he both said and pantomimed, "we will *all* die."

The tribal elder jabbed his spear at Stel and nodded to Antonio. Slowly, Stel handed Antonio the other half of the sacred stone.

"Fine, I trust you will walk me through this later, though." Stel eyed Antonio, who nodded in return. "Now, what do we do with it?" Stel asked.

Antonio pointed up, out of the pit. "We take it away from here. Right now, let's go." He found his backpack on the floor of the pit and picked it up. It was none the worse for wear, so he dusted it off and put the half-meteorite that came from the Amazon back inside. As soon as he did, both rock-halves changed their color from red to orange. He shouldered the pack and adjusted the straps in preparation for the ascent out of the pit.

"What about the one that was already here?" Stel asked, pointing to the sacred stone glowing at their feet.

"We leave it," Antonio said. "It belongs here. Just not next to the other one. Let's go."

Stel looked to the tribal members, who in turn pointed up. He and Antonio nodded, and the tribe began to scale the rocky wall toward the top of the pit. Stel watched as Antonio tested his first footholds on the wall.

"You going to be okay with that heavy pack?" Stel asked.

Antonio looked back at his backpack, now glowing a duller orange. He nodded.

"I think if this thing was going to kill me, it would have done so already."

CHAPTER 28

Stel reached the top of the pit first and scrambled out. Antonio, both burdened with the heavy pack and mentally drained from his inexplicable puzzle-solving session with his father, was slower to reach the rim of the subterranean depression, but he managed to pull himself up and over the lip onto the wider cavern floor. The natives were all up already, collecting their arrows and drinking water from a narrow creek that flowed through here. But there was a noise growing in intensity, something not part of the jungle.

Antonio couldn't see the sky, but he knew what it was all the same. A helicopter, coming this way. He brought his gaze back down to look at Stel, to see if he had anything to say about it, when he froze in place.

Stel had a small pistol pointed right at Antonio's chest.

"I don't know what went on down there, Antonio, but I don't trust you anymore after your little disappearing act. I'm taking this artifact."

Antonio shook his head slowly. "Obviously the meteorites have powers we don't yet comprehend. They should be studied by the greater scientific community, Stel. As a scientist, you know this! Let the world benefit from knowing what they are and how they work. What are you going to do with it, anyway?"

"Do with *them*, you mean?" Slowly, Stel's gaze travelled from Antonio to the pit.

Antonio exhaled sharply, his eyes narrowing. "You plan to take both halves? Are you crazy?"

"Maybe just a little." Stel's eyes flashed defiance.

The helicopter was louder now, no doubt preparing to land just outside the cavern. "That's my ride," Stel said, jerking his head toward the cavern exit. "You play nice, Antonio, and you'll be fine. Just hike on out of here and go on about your life, don't try to be a hero."

"And if I don't?"

Stel chuckled softly as he nodded to the pit.

"An air unit strike team is coming for the other stone. You have just enough time to get out of here safely if you go now. Leave this place and don't come back. I can't guarantee your safety if you do."

Stel looked at his watch and turned around toward the exit as he heard the helo's motor change pitch, indicating it had landed on the forest floor. Antonio watched as Stel began moving toward the exit. Antonio followed him, but at a slower pace, until they reached the aperture in the rock that led out into the stream.

By the time Antonio, and the tribal men behind him, emerged from the cavern, Stel was jumping into the helicopter, which had landed in the stream bed itself. The only other person Antonio could see inside was the pilot, who lifted off immediately while Stel moved up front and took the co-pilot seat.

The aircraft hovered above the canopy for a couple of seconds, Stel looking down on Antonio, watching him.

And then the pilot put the craft into gear, and off it raced over the rain forest.

CHAPTER 29

Antonio hung his head in shame when the helicopter had disappeared from sight, the rumble of its engine now fading into the distance. How could he have been so stupid? How could he have trusted Stel like he had? He mentally replayed the highlights of his recent interactions with his former rival, now of course realizing that the rivalry was anything but former. *He'd probably intended to use me from the moment I contacted him,* Antonio thought. But he had been the one who first reached out to Stel, so for that he had only himself to blame. He had been greedy, wanting to be first to publish in the journals but knowing he needed an anthropologist on board to ensure acceptance…and for that he had paid the price.

Antonio looked up and saw the tribal members gathered around him, the confused, concerned expressions on their painted faces. He was trying to think of what to say to them, out of the very limited amount of words he now knew in their language, when again the most unnatural sound of a helicopter echoed across the jungle. Antonio recalled Stel's words about a strike team with a shiver.

Or maybe it's Stel coming back, having changed his mind about what he's doing? Antonio knew that the wishful thought was just that when a sleek military chopper, much larger than the one that had picked up Stel, flew into view across the rain forest. Strike team.

Antonio pointed into the pit. "They're coming for the sacred stone!" He said it in English just to get their attention, and then took precious seconds to translate it for them to the best of his ability. The tribe's reaction was to hold up their spears and arrows. Tracking the helicopter with them as it moved across the sky. This was how they dealt with the other helicopters they'd seen, Antonio thought, but in this case they had no idea how little it would matter.

He shook his head at them. Pantomimed gunfire after pointing at the approaching helo. Pointed down to the pit again, and then mimicked carrying the meteorite, and pointed off into the jungle, where not even a game trail penetrated. He tried the tribal words he thought meant "run" and "hide," then again pointed to the incoming aircraft and acted out shooting a gun. He was sure they knew what guns were since Stel had told him about their run-ins with the Indian coast guard and other parties.

Antonio was pleased to see one of the men, and only one, scramble to the pit. He was the best climber, too, he thought. Good. This would need to be fast. He nodded to him and waved him on. "Go! Get it! Yes! Hurry!"

The native dropped down into the pit and Antonio immediately turned to the half-dozen other men, people he would somehow need to coordinate if they were going to escape with the sacred stone. He pointed to an ordinary boulder on the ground, ran to it and picked it up. Then he scuttled to the very edge of the pit and dropped it there. Antonio thought that maybe if the mercenaries entered the pit looking for the sacred stone, that they would be able to push the heavy rocks down on them. The natives eyed him with uncertainty, until he pointed to another nearby rock, and another, then another. He himself ran to a different rock and carried it to the edge of the pit. Then one of the tribesman got with the program and ran to a rock, made eye contact with Antonio, who nodded vigorously, then carried it to the edge of the pit as Antonio had done. After that, the floodgates opened and all of the tribe members deposited stones in a ring around the sacred pit.

By the time they were done, the one who had descended into the pit emerged with the sacred stone. He was helped over the new rim of rocks by his tribe, and then Antonio waved to get their attention. He tried the word for "fast," hoping he had picked it up somewhere along the way. He said the word with the inflection of a question, while pointing in turn at the tribesmen. Immediately, they all pointed to one man in the middle. Good, Antonio thought, he'd gotten the right word. The individual was tall and rangy, with a runner's body. He looked fast.

Antonio indicated that they should give him the stone, and that he needed to run with it as fast as he could to hide it somewhere safe.

The helo hovered nearby, as if looking for them, and then moved slowly toward them, low over the trees. Then they heard a male voice, speaking English, though a loud-hailer: "Dr. Antonio Medina and team: remain where you are and no one will get hurt. We just need to talk."

Antonio nearly laughed out loud. *Just need to talk?* Who flies in with two helicopters-- one to extract your supposed business partner, and one to come back to "talk?"

He looked at the man with the sacred stone and said "go" with an accompanying hand gesture. Then he turned to the rest of the tribe and pointed to the foliage closest to the pit. He looked to the helicopter and saw men in camo-green jumpsuits with automatic rifles slung over their backs fast-roping out of it. *What in God's name?* Someone with powerful connections meant business when it came to stealing the artifacts, that was easy enough to see.

Realizing there was no time for his painfully slow communications, he led by example and dove into the nearest stand of plants. Then he stuck his head out and beckoned them toward him, hoping they'd get the idea. Antonio listened but couldn't hear the soldiers, or mercenaries, or whoever they were hit the ground over the noise of the helicopter. He knew they were on the way, though, and fast, so he was extremely thankful to see the tribal people take his cue and leap into the surrounding bushes.

He only hoped they would stay hidden long enough for his crazy plan to work. The hairs on his arms stood on end as he crouched lower in his green shroud. He told himself this was the dumbest idea he'd ever come up with in his life, that he should have taken Stel's parting advice and simply ran away. But it was too late for that now, as the first of the armed mercenaries came running into the pit area.

The warrior who entered the tiny clearing was decked from head to toe in military camo, including a balaclava that covered his face. Antonio looked but couldn't see any kind of identifier on the uniform, if that's what it is—no flag, no insignia, name, nothing. What was clear was that the guy was geared up with multiple guns, knives, extra magazines…and a radio, which he brought to his lips as he approached the pit. He cautiously leaned over the lip of it, while saying, "Think I got something here. Right over by—"

Antonio saw his chance and took it. He sprang from the bushes and barreled toward the interloper, knowing he would hear him but counting on the fact that he would reach him in time. He lowered his shoulder as he'd been taught to do in high school football practice, and slammed into the mercenary just as he'd almost brought his submachine gun all the way around.

Antonio had one panicky moment of absolute, unbridled fear, where his foe gripped him on the arm and he thought he was going to be dragged over the edge of the pit with him. But at the last second he was able to brush him off as the shocked, horrified look in the man's falling eyes burned itself into Antonio's memory forever. The fall was not survivable, and the mercenary added his corpse to that of the tribal man who'd succumbed to the pit's gravitational forces earlier.

Antonio had no time to celebrate his small victory, however, because the rumble of foliage nearby, from the same direction the last mercenary had come, told him that more soldiers would be here momentarily. He'd won the first battle but by no means the war.

One of the tribal members' heads poked out of a bush, and Antonio frantically motioned for him to conceal himself again. He did, and Antonio slipped into the greenery beside him, just as three more mercenaries came into view.

Two carried pistols at the ready while one had an automatic rifle slung over one shoulder as he talked into a handheld radio, saying, "…have a visual on you yet, we're--hold on, got something."

Antonio knew that he would need the tribe's help with these three, no way could he handle them all on his own. He tapped the one next to him on the shoulder and pointed. That man nodded, then tapped the one next to him. Then Antonio leapt from the bushes, committing himself to the surprise attack. He was relieved to hear the leaves ruffle as the rest of the tribe followed suit.

Seven men all told—Antonio and the half-dozen indigenous warriors—charged the three mercenaries as a group. The gang tackle was messy, with Antonio not being able to see exactly what happened. All he knew was that he and one other tribal man were first to reach the gunmen, who swiveled around while bringing their firearms to bear. He head-butted the middle man while wrapping an arm around each of the other two. He didn't think this was going to be as effective as with the first single warrior, and he was right. Immediately he felt the butt of a rifle skid across his forehead. Warm liquid trickled down his face, even though it was only a glancing blow--a miss, basically--compared to the intention, which was to smash him in the temple and knock him out.

Still, the warrior in the middle yelled as he was thrust over the edge of the pit, his voice growing hollow as it echoed on the way down until it was suddenly cut short. Antonio would not have been able to handle the remaining two mercenaries, there was no doubt about that. But the six oncoming tribesmen meant that they had to devote their attention to protecting themselves rather than throwing Antonio to his death.

Three tribesmen landed on the unknown soldier to the left, shifting and bending as they dragged him to the edge. He wasn't going down without a fight, though, and managed to get off two rounds from his handgun as he flew over the lip to his messy death below. One of those rounds struck a tribal man in the neck, which he clutched with both hands as he gurgled softly into suffocation amid the remainder of the melee.

The surviving mercenary, now faced with a six-on-one fight, recognized that even with a machine gun he was woefully out-forced at such close quarters. He turned and attempted to leap across part of the open pit in order to reach an open patch of ground from which to either stage an automatic fire attack or run away. His jump came up short, however, and his lead foot missed the edge, causing his head to slap into the side of the pit while his hands grasped the edge. He started to pull himself back up but a tribe member reached him far too soon, eyes wide while he stamped on the man's hands with his bare heel until he dropped away forever.

Antonio looked around but saw no one else coming. He could hear the helicopter hovering nearby. How many more men could have been deployed from it? He shook his head. *Four mercenaries killed, plus one tribal warrior in this battle.* There was no going back from this now. He had to operate on the assumption that more mercenaries were coming. What to do? He racked his brain for a plan while looking around the area until an idea sparked.

He picked up one of the large rocks that they had deposited on the edge of the pit. It was approximately the same size as the sacred stone, and Antonio made a show of running with it. He picked up another rock and showed the tribe how they should each get one. By the time they had each gathered a (non-sacred) stone, Antonio heard the helo suddenly become louder. He looked up to see it directly over the pit clearing, three more soldiers fast-roping out of it. Antonio at least had a plan—for each of them to carry a fake rock into the jungle and split up, so that the mercenaries wouldn't know who had the real stone. But their physical skills were about to be put to the test. Of that he had little doubt.

"Go! Go!" He waved both hands outward while turning in a circle.

The tribe took off running as instructed and then Antonio started, but halted, realizing that he forgot to pick up his own dummy stone. He snatched it up off the ground and ran off in one of the more dangerous routes toward the helicopter, wanting to draw attention away from the real 'keeper of the stone' as Antonio thought of him now, who ran in the opposite direction.

He began to run himself, to the right, along the game path. The rock slowed him down considerably and he had to fight his very strong instinct to simply ditch it and run faster. But he suppressed that urge and told himself to carry out the plan as his brain had logically made it a few minutes ago, under comparably less stress.

The next thing he heard was the chopper lifting off again. It didn't fly away, though, but hovered above the canopy, no doubt providing an eye in the sky for its foot soldiers, pointing out where their targets were going. Antonio ran into the jungle, knowing he was making a lot of noise as he crashed through plants and pounded his feet on the earth, but figuring the helo noise for now would cover him until his pursuers got very close.

He lamented that he didn't have time to communicate a plan with the tribe as to when and where they would meet up again, but as bursts of machine gun fire reverberated through the jungle, he knew he'd done the best thing by getting them moving right away. These people from the helicopter, whoever they were, were not messing around.

Antonio stayed within the heaviest jungle cover, lugging his decoy rock. After a few minutes during which he heard sporadic gunfire and the occasional guttural yell, he decided to head in the direction the tribal man with the genuine stone had run off in. But as he spun around in frantic circles, leaves and branches smacking his face, he saw that he had no idea of which way to go. Looking up, he saw a tree that would be easily climbable. If he set down the fake stone, that is.

He dropped the rock at the base of the tree and started to climb. He tried to disturb the branches as little as possible so as not to give away his position, but some motion was inevitable. As he climbed he blocked out the stress of wondering whether a volley of automatic weapons fire would cut him down at any moment, by thinking about where the keeper of the sacred stone would be taking the artifact.

He had seen him run toward the mountain, toward the waterfall basically, but that was it. He had nothing more to go on. He kicked himself for not taking the time to work that out better, but then his head was poking through the leaves and he had a partial view of his surroundings. The canopy ceiling was still much farther above him, but this was enough to see that the mountain was off to his left, and right now that was all he needed. He could hear the helo hovering somewhere in the vicinity, but couldn't see it.

Antonio spider-monkeyed his way down the tree, making sure not to land on the ground with a loud thump. He scooped up his decoy rock and set out through the thick jungle toward the mountain. It seemed like a long time that he pushed his way through the tangle of greenery, and after a while he heard no more sounds of battle. He wasn't sure if that was a good or a bad sign, but he kept on making his way to the verdant cliff where the keeper of the stone had gone.

He fell back on his thoughts while he trudged through the snarled rain forest, pausing here and there to swat at a massive insect or part thorny vines. Where would the tribal man take the sacred stone now that it was out of the pit? Antonio envisioned the tribe's surroundings as if he was an eagle flying above. The jungle, the waterfall, the mountain...any of those places could offer numerous hiding places, Antonio, knew. But which one to check first? And would the man stay with the stone where he brought it? Not likely, Antonio thought. He'd probably stash it somewhere and then return to his village.

The village!

That's where he should go to rendezvous with the tribe, to get an update of where the stone was taken. He had no better idea than that, at any rate. He took stock of his position, the mountain on his right, the waterfall some distance behind him, and the thick rain forest off to his left. The village was in front of him, a three day hike away. Three days of travelling the jungle with no gear by himself. But he could think of no better alternative, so he started moving in that direction, smiling when he came across some landmark he recognized from the trip up here, because it meant he was going the right way.

CHAPTER 30

Three days later
Andaman Islands

Antonio splashed his face with stream water before standing and surveying his surroundings. Only another mile or so and he would reach the tribal village. On his trek here, he'd seen no other humans. He did hear a chopper once, far in the distance, but had no idea where it was going or even if it was one of Stel's. He'd thought a lot about Stel, too, especially while sleeping in the same treetop campsites, reliving their conversations. And to think he'd thought they'd almost become friends. It made him angry with himself, but all he could do at this point was to move on; there was no point in second-guessing things now.

As Antonio walked briskly toward the village, it occurred to him that he hadn't actually been to it before. He and Stel had landed by helicopter on the mudflat (he was good at procuring helo's wasn't he?), and then immediately trekked past the village to the place of the sacred stone. He now recognized many sights, specific groupings of trees, rock formations, branching footpaths, however, and so he knew he was almost to the tribe's home.

For some reason he also thought of his father's final home, in a village not unlike this one, but on the other side of the world, with a pang of sadness. His father had helped that tribe guard this same secret, though, and so it gave Antonio pride to be helping to safeguard it from Stel's outside forces. For whatever reason they wanted the artifacts, it was contrary to what his father had wished.

Antonio rounded a clump of trees and felt a swelling of anticipation as he laid eyes on the final approach to the village. He could see a wide path leading to an open area, a few huts grouped inside. He'd made it! He started to run, anxious to see if the bearer of the stone had made it here. He'd seen no sign of his passage along the way, but he knew the tribal people usually didn't leave much trace of their passing. It did seem odd to him that he hadn't seen any villagers yet, since usually they kept sharp lookouts, and tribe members would be out nearby foraging and going about their daily business. But so far he'd seen absolutely no one. Maybe they're all inside the village listening to stories from the stone bearer. It must be quite a shock for the rest of the tribe to suddenly see their sacred object exposed in the middle of their settlement, after all. And how long could the tribal man have gotten here ahead of me, Antonio thought? He supposed most of a full day.

But as Antonio entered the village, his heart sank.

The bodies lay everywhere. Each had been riddled with bullets. It was obvious they'd been laid to waste from above, riddled with machine gun fire from the helicopter. Antonio suppressed the urge to vomit as long as he could because he wanted to run to each person and see if there were any survivors, but after he reached the first one—a man who had been in the prime of life—he knelt in the dirt and vomited.

Although he was sure what he would find, Antonio checked the pulse of every single slaughtered man, woman and child in that village. It took nearly an hour, and there were no survivors. He walked around a long house, hoping to find survivors hiding behind it, but there was no one. He had no doubt the mercenaries would have taken no chances, shooting up the entire community to eradicate the living.

Walking back around to the front side of the longhouse, Antonio came across an area he'd missed, an enclosed area cordoned off by bamboo fencing. It was to keep livestock animals inside, but the gate had been opened and whatever had been inside—probably boars or goats, Antonio speculated, had already left. Inside, however, were two more mangled bodies.

Antonio checked the pulse of the first and found him dead of obvious gunshot wounds. The second had succumbed to massive trauma, too, but when he flipped him over to feel for a pulse nonetheless, he nearly had a heart attack on seeing the man's face.

The runner he'd entrusted with the sacred stone!

He was dead, but then….Antonio whirled around as he looked about the space.

Where is the stone?

He rolled the body completely over to make sure he couldn't be laying on top of it somehow, but no, only smooth dirt lay beneath him. Antonio probed the dirt with a stick to make sure it hadn't been buried right where he lay, a last act of defiance before being ripped apart by a hail of lead, but only Earth lay below. Could he have brought the stone all the way here only to have it taken from him while his entire village was slaughtered? Antonio hung his head in shame and sorrow, racked with grief over the senseless violence the artifact had brought down upon them.

He stepped out of the enclosure, not wanting to wallow in the defeat, needing to move in order to think straight. The facts were clear: unless the tribal stone carrier had deposited the stone in some other hiding spot before he had come here, then Stel's team had taken it in violently spectacular fashion. Antonio wiped a tear from his eye as he looked about the destroyed village. For all their fierceness, their unconventional ways, he remembered how ultimately accepting this uncontacted tribe had been to him, doing their best to explain things about their world to Antonio and Stel despite the language barrier. His gaze roved over them as he flashed on his interactions with the villagers, sleeping in the trees, hiking along the paths, coming to the sacred stone in the pit…

And then his gaze alighted on a hut with a vine-framed doorway in the middle of the communal open space. There was something about that building, but what was it? Antonio walked slowly towards it while he recollected. By the time he reached it, he knew what to check.

He entered the crudely hewn structure, cringing at the dead woman inside. He had already checked her pulse and found her dead. It was a feature of the space itself he was interested in at the moment. Antonio gently dragged the woman's dead body away from the center of the floor, eyeing the woven grass mats that covered the dirt. He pulled the mats aside and gasped as a crude trapdoor made of thin logs was revealed.

He opened the door and caught his breath.

Just like that, there it was. Sitting in the center of the space, the half-meteorite was not glowing.

Instantly, he understood what must have happened when the runner they had all entrusted to hide the stone had reached the village. He must have known that attack was imminent, possibly watching with terror as the helicopter raced past him looking for his village, and so had sought a quick hiding place. So he had stashed the stone in the hidey-hole beneath the mat, no doubt the tribe's equivalent of a safe for valuables.

And the move had worked, for the stone was still here.

Antonio reached out and put a hand on it. It began to glow a dull orange, like the dying embers of a doused campfire. He shrugged off his backpack and, once again, loaded the sacred stone into it. He was all too aware that carrying this artifact around was a death sentence now, but at the same time, so many people had already died for it that he felt a duty to the tribe—to both tribes, really-- to protect it.

He shouldered his loaded pack and stood in the doorway to the hut, looking out. *Now what?* He needed to get out of here, off the island and back to…to America, he supposed. With the artifact. He could use his satellite phone to call the boat for pickup, as had been the plan, but because the boat service had been arranged by Stel, he no longer trusted it. He would have to get himself off of the Andaman Islands and to the Indian mainland, first, then to America after that, on his own.

Regardless of how that happened, Antonio mused, he would need to hike from here to the beach and the mud flats--that much was true no matter what happened after that. So he walked out of the hut, took one last look at the dead villagers, bowed his head in a moment of prayer, and then left the village.

CHAPTER 31

By the time Antonio had trekked about halfway from the village to the beach, he was ready to make his first phone call. He'd been moving at a good clip, nearly a jog the entire way, and so he was satisfied enough with his progress to take a rest. Not to mention he had arrangements to make. He found a slanted tree trunk to sit on while he drank water from cup-shaped leaves that had collected during the last rain. He looked around at the forest while he thought about who to call, listening to the twittering of birds, the drone of insects and the unseen activity that caused branches to crack and leaves to crackle. To his practiced ears, it sounded similar to the Amazon, and yet he was sure that if he closed his eyes while listening to recordings of both forests, that he would be able to distinguish them.

You knew you were an ecologist when you could tell apart the different forests by sound alone, Antonio thought with a sigh. You knew you'd been in the game a long time when you got to that point. Maybe it was time to hang it up after this, he considered with a twinge of sadness. Or at least cut back to teaching only, no more field research. After this he wasn't sure he could ever handle visiting the jungle again, especially seeing a tribe.

But those were things to think about later. Right now he still had a situation to deal with, notably getting off this island with an artifact that someone was willing to commit what was tantamount to genocide for. He turned his sat-phone over in his hands as he thought about his next move. He decided that he'd rather get to the beach before trying to arrange transportation. He wasn't entirely sure his phone calls couldn't be tracked, if not the conversation itself, then simply the radio signals which could be used to triangulate his position as they bounced around various satellites and receivers.

But the stickier problem was what to do with the artifact in his backpack. He couldn't very well keep this thing forever. Stel's hit men would seek him out when they did make it down to the pit and couldn't find it. He imagined them torturing him to pry the whereabouts of the stone from him, thinking maybe that he knew where the tribe had hidden it. Shivering, he scrolled through the pitifully short contact list in his sat-phone. A few work colleagues, mostly, including Stel, he noted with a sour frown. He needed some sort of serious help with this, maybe even government intervention.

*Government...*He had a few Brazilian government contacts, including President Rocha now, but he was in India, and he knew absolutely no one here. It was Stel's domain, not his. Then there was his government, but why would it be the U.S. government's problem? Why would they care? He thought about this while watching the sun's rays filter through the trees. The artifact represented unknown technology. As such, it was something they'd want to learn from. Not only that, it came embedded in a meteorite, which meant it could have originated from space. If they wanted an inside track into obtaining a first look at what might possibly be alien technology, then they would need to help Antonio locate Stel and the half-rock device he stole.

Antonio nodded to himself as his eye caught on one of the names in his contact list.

James Duncan.

Duncan was his main grant administration contact with the National Science Foundation. He was the guy Antonio dealt with whenever he had to apply for a new grant. They'd worked together in that capacity for most of the last ten years. Antonio tried to think of who else he knew in government, but after another minute of searching both his phone and his brain, he had to conclude that Duncan was it.

He didn't know what the NSF man would be able to do, if anything, but he figured the NSF would like to be the first to know about any potential research projects involving the artifact. It was either that, he mused, or else try cold-calling the White House or the Pentagon and explaining his situation. He was less than confident that route would produce positive results anytime soon, so he decided to start with Duncan and take it from there.

He placed a call to his NSF contact and waited while it rang. After a few rings the familiar nasal whine came through Antonio's speaker. "James Duncan here."

"Good afternoon, James," Antonio began, mentally calculating the time zone difference. It was very late afternoon there, 5:00 or 6:00, but close enough. He was lucky to have caught him before he left for the day. "Antonio Medina here."

"Dr. Medina, to what do I owe the pleasure of your call? New grant application coming my way, I suppose?"

"You could say that. But it's more complicated than that. And potentially much more rewarding."

"You've got my interest piqued enough to pour one more cup of coffee from this newfangled espresso maker we got in the office. If the taxpayers only knew. So tell me about it while I brew up a mocha Frappuccino."

Antonio told him the entire story from the beginning. By the time he'd finished Duncan had made a second caffeinated beverage. "Jesus, Antonio. And you're still there now, in the Andamans? Are you in danger?"

"I can get myself out of here, James, don't worry about that. But what I need from you is help in stopping Dr. Foster, because it doesn't matter where in the world I am if they think I have the other half of the artifact. And I do. So what I need from you is—"

"To look into Stel's funding sources, right?"

Normally being interrupted was a pet peeve of Antonio's, but this time he appreciated the expediency. "Correct."

"Okay, it's a routine matter for me to look up in our own databases what funding he's received recently…" Antonio heard the rapid-fire clacking of computer keys. "Hmmm, that's a little odd."

"What's odd? Not that I don't enjoy chatting, James, but I'm on a satellite phone here in the middle of nowhere, and when my battery dies, that's it, unless we can shout across two oceans and the Gulf of Mexico."

"Understood. It seems that not only has Foster had zero NSF funding in the last eight years, but in the past five he's had zero public--that is government--funding of any kind."

"He's got a steady publication history, though, so he must be getting funding from somewhere."

"Right, but it's private. Hold on, searching another database…Okay, here we go. He's been funded exclusively by a private company called International Semiconductor, Incorporated."

"International Semi? Don't they make computer chips?"

"Yeah. They're in everything. Probably even in that phone you're talking to me on right now."

Antonio looked at his device. "Great. Listen, James, you're the only contact I have in the government. I know this might be a little above your pay grade, so to speak, but I really need help with getting the other half of this meteorite artifact back from Stel or whoever Stel gave it to."

"Doing that is way beyond my job description, but if I can establish a link between Dr. Foster's lab and some kind of wrongdoing that has to do with misrepresentation of funding or something along those lines, I may be able to pass it up the chain, and then it'll be in their hands."

"Check into the computer lab he works with, too. They're the ones who actually had possession of the first half of the artifact, the ones who came up with the simulation theory. Dr. James Hanlan. There was a geology lab at Oxford involved, too."

"Will do. That's enough homework to keep me busy for a little while, Antonio. You better get off the horn and get yourself home. I'll contact you when I have results."

"As soon as you can, James. Thanks. I'll be sure to come up with a suitable gift a government bureaucrat would appreciate."

"Get out of jail free cards are always welcome. Good luck." Antonio ended the call and returned the phone to his pocket. Time to get back on the trail. With a last look around at the forest, he continued on toward the beach.

CHAPTER 32

Antonio splashed across the shallow lagoon. He'd lost his sunglasses somewhere along the way and cursed at the blinding tropical sun reflecting off the water. He'd picked a route that was further to the left, facing out to sea, than he'd gone before, and now he found himself having to pick his way carefully through a small garden of corals. Large torpedo-shaped, silver fish darted here and there as he shuffled his feet across the sandy areas to avoid stepping on a stingray, and high-stepped between the corals and sponges to avoid scraping his ankles.

He'd scouted the entire vista from the cover of the jungle before venturing out onto the mud flats, and had seen no one. No people, tribal or otherwise--no boats, no planes, absolutely nothing. Out on the mud flats he'd be closer to any boats that did happen to come along, so he opted to wait out there. He stepped out of the lagoon up onto the mud flat, softer near the edge and turning hard packed a few feet in.

He still didn't trust Stel's boat pilot, as much as he wanted to give him a call and say he was ready to be picked up. He imagined Stel would have him on standby, just in case he was stupid enough to contact him. No, he'd just have to find his own way out of here. And fast, too, he realized, turning around to scan the beach where he'd seen the tribe run out of the jungle to attack them when they'd landed via helo. The village had been decimated, but the hunting party that he'd gone with to the sacred stone pit—they were still out there somewhere, and after the strike team hit, they might have come back to the village. Were they to see him here after what had happened, he couldn't be sure they wouldn't take revenge by killing him on the spot. The language wall between them would be too great to try and explain what had transpired between him and Stel.

Antonio turned back around and stared out to sea. How had he gotten himself into this mess? He never should have called Stel. But it was too late for that kind of thinking now. He had set this chain of events into motion and now he had a responsibility to make it right.

His thoughts were interrupted by the sound of a rumbling, throaty engine. He looked up from the burrowing clam he'd been staring at and out to sea. He scanned left to right until he spotted a fishing trawler chugging along from the open ocean toward the Indian mainland. Antonio shot to his feet. He bolted to the edge of the mud flat, the Andaman Sea representing a chasm between him and the Indian continent.

The vessel was still far off, a couple of miles or so, but he knew it would have to pass within decent visual range of the flat for it to continue on its current course, since a shallow coral reef created a navigable channel. But what was the best way to make himself seen to the boat? He had no flares, no radio, no way to start a fire…Antonio eyeballed the mudflat, looking for nothing specific, just anything that might give him an idea. Finally, on the lagoon-facing edge of the flat he spotted a tree branch that had been freshly washed up, judging by the fact that it still had green leaves on it.

He ran to it and picked it up. It was a good twenty-feet long. He broke off a couple of peripheral, smaller branches that made it unwieldy, and then he tried hoisting it into the air. He found he was able to stick it straight up and wave it back and forth, a good twenty-five feet or so into the air combined with his height.

He ran with it to the ocean edge of the mud flat and waited for the trawler to approach. Antonio knew that during long sea voyages, sailors didn't always have someone watching to see what was around them, other than potential navigation hazards, so spotting a man standing on a distant mud flat or sandbar was not a given. But in this case, the reputation of the Andaman Islands tribes was well-known, and so he gave it good odds that they would be looking his way. In fact, he thought, raising his tree branch into the air, he had to be careful he wasn't mistaken for a tribal member himself and shot at.

Antonio waved the tree branch back and forth as the trawler neared. He started to run back and forth along the mud bank to hopefully make himself even more visible with added motion. His arms burned with the effort, but he willed himself to keep at it, knowing that this fishing boat was his best chance of leaving this island anytime soon.

He had just resigned himself to the unsavory reality that the boat was going to pass him right by, when the cadence of the engines changed and the prow of the vessel turned toward the mudflat. Antonio lifted a booted foot out of the muck, dredging up a large clam with it. He eyed the mollusk, thinking about how he would probably need to eat these raw while he waited for another ship to come along unless he could make this opportunity work.

Suddenly two bright flashes of light appeared from the bridge of the vessel. They were signaling him! He stood in place and dropped the branch, waving both arms above his head instead. No doubt they would be extremely wary of approaching, suspecting a trap, of being lured to the mudflat only to be attacked by the rest of the tribe hidden just inside the forest behind the beach. But he persisted with movements he knew were uncharacteristic of tribal people, decidedly western gestures, even when seen from a distance.

The fishing boat continued to approach the mudflat at a slow pace. Encouraged, Antonio continued his show of needing help, waving his arms in an X pattern, then running to a different place and doing the same thing. When he was certain that he had been seen, he stood in place and watched the boat as it neared.

The vessel was old, rust streaked, but clearly very functional, its decks stacked with nets, crates, cranes, winches and other machinery. He could see a few crew members going about their working business on the aft deck, while some others were lined up against the port rail, looking in his direction. He heard a voice over a loudspeaker but couldn't make out what it was saying. It was taking the right action, though, he could see that, so he stood and waited, trying to project as peaceful a demeanor as possible.

At last the craft was close enough to shore that they could shout to him through a megaphone. The sentence was in Indian, but Antonio recognized a single word: *help*. He raised a hand high and shouted, "Yes!" A minute passed during which Antonio began to think they didn't believe him, that they were going to head back out to sea without him. But then he heard a splash as a tender vessel was launched. Shortly after that he heard the whine of a small outboard motor, and then two men riding the dinghy rode up onto the mudflat, about fifty feet away from him. No doubt they wanted to give themselves one final chance to assess him, to see whether he posed a threat.

"Hi, do you speak English?" Antonio called out when they stepped from the dinghy onto the flat.

"Yes," one of them, an Indian man who was thinner and taller than his fellow crewman said. "How did you get here?"

Antonio explained with as little detail as possible that he was a scientific researcher who had become separated from his expedition team. They had already been picked up, he lied, but due to an erroneous head count, they hadn't realized they were short a man when the boat left the island.

After more conversation, the crew made the decision that he was trustworthy enough to take aboard. He was given a hammock in a shared crews' quarters, and during the two-days' passage to the Indian mainland, he passed the time regaling the crew with tales of the natives and the island itself. He slept a lot, too, surprised at how exhausted his ordeal had made him. He awoke from such a slumber to find that the vessel was docking in a harbor.

Antonio gathered his backpack—he'd slept with it to keep the artifact safe—thanked the crew and captain and walked onto the Indian continent.

CHAPTER 33

Mumbai, India

The sheer density of crowds on the sidewalk and the traffic in the streets was shocking to Antonio as he strolled along the avenue. It was his first trip here, and the chaotic mish-mash of cars, bikes, lorries, motorcycles, and pedestrians was disorienting, especially after being in the jungle for days. After being dropped off at a wharf by the fishing boat, he'd taken a bus across the country to the city of eighteen million. There were closer cities and towns along his route where he could have stopped to rest, but he needed access to very modern technology for what he had in mind—for starters, a cell-phone signal.

He heard his smartphone ring for the first time since he'd left with Stel in the helicopter. He glanced at the caller ID and saw that it was James Duncan, his NSF contact. "Talk to me, James. You find anything out?"

"Where are you by the way?"

"I'd better not say." Antonio shifted the weight of his pack on his back as he threaded his way through the thick sidewalk crowd. "But I'm safe for now, off the island."

"You've got cell reception, at least, wherever you are. I'll get right to the point. I called in a few favors and got our investigative unit to fast-track this little issue."

Antonio paused to let three kids sharing one bicycle pass him by. "The NSF has an investigative unit?"

"Kind of a little-known fact, but yeah. Normally this wouldn't make it across their desk, either, but like I said—favors. And after they see what I dug up, I've got a feeling they may want to throw some resources at this, Antonio. But before we get too far—I know we're short on time—let me tell you this: There are some powerful people after this artifact or whatever it is."

"Politicians? Black market dealers? Who?"

"Let's start with your man, Stel Foster."

"Okay."

"It sure is noisy wherever the hell you are."

Antonio did his best to shield the phone from the blaring horn of a bus trying to make its way through a throng of people and horses. "Big city. Nice change of pace from where I've been, though, I'm not complaining. So tell me more."

Duncan continued. "This company that's been funding Foster's research—International Semi?"

"What about it?"

"Strange bird, it is. It's set up like a global conglomerate, with sub-holdings and subsidiaries all over the place from all the major cities—maybe even the one you're in now, who knows—to assorted backwater towns pretty much no one's heard but the people who live there."

"Is there something wrong with that?"

"It makes it harder to figure out where all the money goes, I can tell you that much, but in and of itself, no. But what is a little odd is that a sizable percentage of holdings from various offshore and numbered accounts can all be traced to one William Vandoven." Duncan paused as if to see whether Antonio would have a reaction.

"Doesn't ring any bells for me."

"He's Chairman of a sort of secret society called The Bilderberg Group."

Antonio coughed as he passed a vendor stall that wafted pungent incense smoke. "I do think I've heard of them—they're like a think tank?"

"Sort of, yeah, formed back in the 1950s. Officially, their goal is to bolster Western European and U.S. relations, but some people say they're really striving to achieve a one-world government."

"So they're trying to take over the world?" Antonio smiled at a passing Indian man who gave him a quizzical look as he spoke the question.

"That's one way to interpret it. And if what we understand about this artifact you found is even half true, it sounds like something that would further their aims."

"So Stel's funding comes from The Bilderberg Group?"

"Yes."

"Is Stel in it?"

"He's not actually a member as far as we can tell, nor is the computer scientist at Oxford whose team decoded the first half of the device—Dr. James Hanlan. I'm still checking into the geologists, but they appear to be uninvolved so far. But we know for sure that both Foster and Hanlan are funded almost exclusively by The Bilderberg Group. It's weird, even though they are both full-time faculty at the university, it's like they're operating as some rogue academic group within the school. Their own funding, their own research, their own schedules."

"*Both* of them?" Antonio reached a small open air café and took a seat at an empty table. "No wonder he jumped to help out so quickly."

"Right, so Antonio: a word of caution. The Bilderberg Group is extremely powerful with many wealthy and connected ties to governments and corporations around the world. If they want the other half of that device—and you know they do—they'll be coming for you."

"Yeah, the airborne jungle strike team kind of gave me that impression."

"I know, I don't need to tell you, but I've got to go on record putting it out there. I'm afraid your safety is in fact in jeopardy as we speak. Maybe you should turn the rock over to us."

Antonio set his pack on the ground, looping a foot through the straps to discourage would-be snatch-and-grabbers. "Turning the rock over to you doesn't get us back the other half of the artifact, though. Besides, there's only one safe place for both of these rocks, James, and that's where we found them. The one I have has to go back to the Amazon, it's its destiny."

There was a pause while Duncan considered this. "You asked me to help on this, Antonio, and I did. But a side-effect of that is that now the NSF knows about this…artifact, as you call it…and they're not simply going to forget about it. You've set something into motion here."

"The assistance is welcome, James. I called you, remember? It was my fault for calling Stel in the first place, but now you're the one I called to try and fix things because I've got nowhere else to turn. Look, we have to get the other rock back from Stel, and keep him from getting this one. Because if they have custody of both halves, James, you know what that means?" The silence on the other end told Antonio to continue. "It means they can destroy the world. They'll put the two halves close enough together to demonstrate the awful power of it, and then they'll threaten everyone into doing their bidding, meeting their demands, or else…"

"They put the stones together, which I'm told destroys the computer simulation which comes from where….space? I mean, how else do you get a computing device embedded in a space rock? But who does it come from? That's one thing we haven't been able to figure out."

"One theory is, it comes from *us*—humans—but in the future. They created a simulation to see how their ancestors evolved and behaved. Another more troubling possibility is that whoever created could decide to end the simulation if they don't like how what they've created is acting."

"But on the other hand, wouldn't it mean that, as long as you have the code, the program could be copied and re-run on a different computer? So we'd all effectively be immortal."

Antonio sighed. "Maybe we should save the philosophy discussion for later, James. I'm a wanted man with this thing, and you're telling me one of the most powerful secret organizations in the world is pulling out all the stops to find me."

"What we need to do is put these guys on the defensive."

"How do we do that?" Antonio asked.

"We need to obtain proof that they're the ones behind the illegal actions to steal the artifacts. International artifact theft actually has real laws with actual teeth, whereas proving they don't have rights to some unknown technology could be a bit trickier."

"Public shaming might work," Antonio agreed. "Maybe you could leak a press release? 'Secretive group slaughters entire tribe of jungle people to steals priceless artifact'—that sort of thing?"

A pause ensued and Duncan's voice came back on the line. "I think we can do a step better than that."

CHAPTER 34

London, England

Stel gawked at the device, already separated from its meteorite half, set up on a lab bench. "Are we ready?" he asked a small phalanx of white-coated lab workers. He looked around at the unfamiliar surroundings. "If there's a problem, we could always go back to Oxford—"

"We're almost ready," the lead scientist said, a German man Stel had never seen before, who dismissed him with a curt wave of the hand. Stel bristled at being treated like some disposable lab tech, but he bit his tongue. He had the sinking feeling that he was no longer running the show when it came to this strange artifact, but the hard truth was that these people still paid his salary. In fact, they owned the entire facility in which the meteorite was now located. Stel had wanted to work at Oxford, out of his own lab, or at least Dr. Hanlan 's computer lab, but the managers from International Semiconductor had insisted on using their own private facility. Stel grew irritated that although they said they were almost ready, no one was moving to get things started with analyzing this new half of the artifact.

"We're waiting for a couple of more people," the German said. No sooner had he completed the sentence than the door to the workshop opened and four men in formal business attire entered. Stel caught his

179

breath as he recognized the Chairman of The Bilderberg Group. The reclusive billionaire businessman was not known for making public appearances, and his whereabouts were usually a matter of speculation. All four men from the Group exchanged brief greetings with their scientists, as well as Stel. Then they told the technicians to proceed and stood back to watch as the artifact's device was connected to a conventional computer, as had been done with the other device at Stel's university.

A scientist nodded to the men in suits. "When we run the simulation on this device, we expect that it will run a program like the one that was executed on the second device." Then he turned to a technician who stood poised with a computer cable running from the device.

"Proceed."

#

Mumbai, India

Antonio paid for his coffee at the counter of the Internet India Café and looked for an open table. He found one inside, next to a wall. He occupied it, and then set up the new laptop he'd purchased on the table. While it booted up, he took the artifact's device, which he'd already separated from the meteorite, from his pack.

He looked around, a little concerned someone might be watching him, but if someone was observing him he couldn't tell. The place was noisy, packed with locals speaking a mix of Hindi and English, with loud Bollywood music blaring from overhead speakers. Antonio removed from his pack a plastic bag from the same store where he'd purchased the laptop. It contained a series of cables and electronic parts that he would need to connect the device to his laptop as he'd seen Stel's computer scientist colleagues do at Oxford.

He placed his backpack on the edge of the table to shield his electronics from view, as well as to hopefully discourage anyone else from sitting at his same table. It took him the better part of twenty minutes to make the connection, during which time he looked around frequently to make sure he wasn't attracting undue attention. But he got it done, satisfied that he had successfully duplicated the connection he had seen performed.

Now it was time to find out if it actually worked.

He picked up his coffee and drank from it while doing his best to act nonchalant. He eyeballed his laptop and confirmed that his computer recognized that it was now connected to an external device. Setting down his drink, Stel smiled as he hovered his finger over the enter button. He looked at the computer's clock, just to give him an idea of how much time would elapse once the simulation started: 2:29 P.M. local time.

Perfect.

Antonio smiled and pressed the button.

#

London, England

"Something's different about this program." The small crowd of scientists, technicians and Bilderberg Group members stared up at the wall mounted monitors. On the screens, many dots filled the display, but as time passed they began blinking out, leaving more and more blank space.

Another tech answered the first. "Right, because with the other one, it started with one pixel and grew exponentially from there. This one starts fully populated and depopulates over time."

Puzzlement reigned as the roomful of interested parties considered the raided jungle artifact. "Let it run," one of the suits said, checking his Rolex.

All of a sudden the device seemed to shift on the tabletop, as if an earthquake was in progress. One of the techs looked down at the bench legs, even kicked one, but the table itself was in fact secure. Nothing else in the room was shaking.

"We're losing the sim." One of the scientists pointed to the monitors, where the simulation images that came from the space rock flickered in and out. A technician reached out to the device.

"Maybe the cable's not fully seated in the—" He broke off mid-sentence when his hand reached the device. Instead of gripping the cord to test if it was snug, his hand passed through the device until it touched the tabletop.

Stel had an uneasy feeling. "I've seen this before," he said, watching the unknown piece of technology transform from a solid object into a confusing dispersion of light. The men from The Bilderberg Group turned to him.

"With the first half of the device?" one of them asked. "I didn't read about that in the report," another added.

Stel shook his head, and with the movement came an overwhelming sense of vertigo, as if he was suddenly very dizzy, his feet not fully connected with the floor. "In the Andaman Islands, down in the pit where the tribe kept their half of the artifact…"

Stel sounded to himself like he was really far away from the Bilderberg guys in a tunnel. As he looked at them, they began to appear less dense, shimmering like holograms.

"The meteorite?" one of them said, asking for clarification that the other stone exhibited the same behavior. But to Stel the word seemed to reverberate around the room, its syllables deconstructed into separate parts so that it came out, "The meet….ee……ee….ee…or…ite-ite-ite…." While at the same time everything around him seemed less concrete.

"Dr. Foster?" *Dr. Foster…Fosterers…Fawwwww…..st….*

Stel spoke, but as if in a dream, his words didn't come out. He wanted to explain to them how in the Andaman pit, it was Antonio himself who had disappeared, not the stone. He remembered how the meteorite he had carried in his backpack—the one from the Amazon—had remained in the pit, while Antonio had disappeared. He had left that account out so as not to seem crazy. He didn't know how to explain it and thought he would be laughed at, and they would make jokes about consuming too many strange tribal ethnobotanical concoctions. But now that he wanted to relate that, the words were like fuzz in his mouth.

"Not…the stone…" *Antonio. It was only Antonio who disappeared, the stone stayed be….hi…nnnnd.*

But when Stel looked over to the stone, he saw only an empty tabletop.

CHAPTER 35

To Antonio the scene was unbelievably lush, so much so that he ignored the glowing red border that framed it all. The scene was an evening one, with a reddish glow from the sun having just set, blending into the red frame. He stood on the edge of a placid pond that was bordered by thick, flowering jungle, with large birds of extraordinary plumage perched all around. A full moon was just beginning to rise above the trees behind him, its silvery light reflecting across the ripples of the water.

On the far side of the pond was a building, a large house or a mansion constructed of stone blocks that were covered with fuzzy green growth. Huge pillars supported a second level forming a veranda at ground level, vines and epiphytic plants draped around the dark entrance. Torches mounted on the front of the edifice flickered in the evening light. He wasn't sure why, but he felt calm, serene, relaxed, as he surveyed the surreal scene.

As before when he had been transported to the simulated world (he didn't know what else to call it), he marveled at the realism of the objects. He reached out and touched a plant, to make sure it wasn't some abstract representation, recoiling upon feeling the waxy leaf on his fingertips. But at the same time, he knew. He knew that this wasn't exactly real, although it would likely have a real outcome. What was he supposed to do here, though? The last time he was in this virtual world, his father had been there, too. But this time, he didn't see—

Antonio whirled around as he heard the voice. "Where are we?"

"Hello, Stel."

"What is this place? How did we get here?" Stel glanced around hectically.

As Antonio had been the first time he'd been encapsulated in a simulation or dream world or alternate reality, whatever it was, Stel was frightened, confused, and a little fascinated all at the same time, Antonio could see.

"I don't really know, Stel. But the more important question is: *why* are we here?"

"How should I know?"

Antonio looked around, slowly, carefully, in no hurry to answer. "There's something we're supposed to do here."

"What is it? I don't recognize this place, do you?"

"Not exactly."

"What do you mean, not exactly?"

Antonio shrugged while he and Stel stared at one another from about twenty feet apart. Both wore the same clothes they'd been wearing before coming here. "It's best if you think about it less as a *place*, Stel, and more as a *game*."

"What kind of game?"

"Like a video game, but one that has a real-world outcome depending on your actions taken in the game."

"How do you know so much?"

A loud birdcall squawked somewhere nearby, causing both men to turn their heads, but there was nothing to see.

"Before, when I disappeared from the pit…:"

"You came here?"

Antonio shook his head slowly. "Not here, the scenery was different. But the important thing was that I had to pass a test, I had to demonstrate that I understood something, and then I was given the knowledge to realize that the two meteorite halves should never be allowed to touch."

Stel stood slack-jawed for a moment before speaking. "That was the first thing you said when you came back into the pit—don't let the stones touch."

Antonio nodded. "But this challenge will be different. The two stones are now separated—although it seems you're doing your best not to keep it that way—so that can't be the goal here. You have the Amazon Stone, I have the Andaman stone."

Realization dawned across Antonio's features. "But I don't have it anymore."

Antonio looked Stel up and down, noting that, like him, he didn't not carry objects of any kind, like a backpack; he had only the clothes on his back. "You don't have it with you in here, but just like I don't have mine, it's because they're still sitting wherever they were right before we entered this…simulation," Antonio finished, looking about.

But Stel's eyes widened in obvious panic. "No! I saw it…" He shook his head, looking for the right word. "*Disappear.* It started to waver and shimmer, sort of like a hologram—sort of like *you* did in the pit—and then I saw it vanish. I watched it disappear, Stel, and so did other people in the room with me."

"Other people, such as members of the Bilderberg Group, perhaps?"

Somewhere nearby they heard the growl of a panther, but wherever it was, it remained hidden.

"I see you've been looking for my half of the artifact."

Antonio's face turned red with rage. "It's not *your* artifact, Stel. You stole it. Neither of them belong to us, they belong to the tribes who were entrusted with their safekeeping long ago. Keeping them from being joined together, which would end the simulation that apparently represents all of our existence."

"You're not the Keeper of the Stones, Antonio, even though you seem to have appointed yourself as such. Experts say they came from space, and therefore they belong to no one…or, if you ask me, to whoever gets them first."

To whoever gets them first… Something clicked in Antonio's mind when he heard that, and at the same time an explosion of fluttering bird wings rent the air as a flock of thousands of birds took to the trees.

"I think I know why we're here, Stel."

Stel looked down from the massive avian flock to make eye contact with his former colleague. "Why?"

"I know where my half-stone is." Antonio had a fleeting thought of his backpack sitting unattended in the Internet India Café, but he supposed time was slowed while he was in the dream world, or some such trick of physics. Whatever the case, he hadn't the time to consider it now. "But you said yours disappeared before your eyes, and the eyes of your entire thieving group."

Stel's eyes narrowed for a moment, but that was quickly overshadowed by the new understanding that filtered through his mind. *So you don't have it anymore.*

Stel said nothing while he stared at Antonio, who waved around about the tropical environs.

"It's somewhere in here, Stel. And like you said, it belongs to whoever gets it first."

CHAPTER 36

Antonio watched Stel slowly backstep away from him, until he turned and ran off into a dense stand of foliage. *Game on.*

The arena in which they found themselves was large enough that if the Amazonian Stone was simply dropped into some patch of thicketed greenery, it would take a long time to come across it. Antonio looked up into the trees, recalling the arboreal camping they'd done. There was no way to rule out that it could be nested up there somewhere, too, he thought. He directed his gaze back to ground level and stared out across the placid pond. Even worse, what if the stone was in *there*, underwater?

He walked to the edge of the pond and looked down into its waters. They were crystal clear, enough to see the bottom in detail, where an assortment of strange aquatic plants reminiscent of something out of a Dr. Seuss book reached toward the waning light. Antonio walked along the edge of the pond, tracing its shape as he stared into its depths, looking for the meteorite. He knelt down once and put his hand in the water, to see if it was real, but it just felt like regular water, a little on the warm side, but not unusually so for a tropical environment. He was just about to withdraw his hand when he heard a splash and looked up to see a sizable crocodile swimming right at him from the middle of the pond.

Antonio yelled in surprise and fright as he sprung to his feet, nearly slipping on the moist soil at the pond's edge. The croc lunged at him but missed as Antonio jumped over its head. He cleared it without touching and then turned around to see what it would do next. The answer came in the form of another lunge, this one with mouth open and teeth clamping around the ecologist's lower leg. He kicked the beast in the eye socket with his booted heel, and it retreated, waddling off at high speed. As he watched, the croc seemed to burrow lower and lower into the mud until it disappeared.

Antonio checked his leg. There was a lot of blood, sluicing down his calf and soaking his sock. He pressed a finger into the jagged open wound and felt the pain. This is real, Antonio thought. *I can get physically hurt in this virtual world.* He had no first aid kid with him, but the wound was not deep, so Antonio rinsed his leg in the pond, knowing that crocodile mouths harbored a ridiculous amount of bacteria, meaning he should probably flush it out. He hoped there weren't any more crocodiles in the pond, and he kept an eye open for them while rinsing the leg, but no more predators came. That done, he continued on his inspection of the pond.

It took him what seemed like a long time, probably an hour, to encircle the body of water while carefully probing its watery sediments with his gaze for the artifact. While he did this, he wondered what Stel was doing, and hoped he wasn't getting lucky enough to stumble across the artifact in the bushes.

When he got back to his starting point on the pond, Antonio felt satisfied the stone did not lay within its depths. So now what? He crouched in the tall grass by the pond's edge and listened for signs of Stel, but his ears were greeted only with the tittering and chirping of birds.

The house loomed in the distance through the jungle, torches flickering in the dying light. Too many questions flooded his mind upon seeing it. What if it's locked? What if it's not real? A trap? It seems so out of place, why is it here? He didn't recognize the building itself from any part of his real life. What if entering it takes him to some other simulation and the stone is here in this one? Yet, short of combing through the foliage and trees for the meteorite, he didn't see any other logical places to look.

Antonio moved toward the structure at a brisk walk, doing his best not to make noise with his passage, but finding it hard not to run straight to the house. At one point he came to a jumble of rocks in a ground depression, and he took the time to comb through these, casting some aside, turning them over, recoiling once as a serpent slithered out from under its dislodged hiding place, but the space rock was not among them.

He kept going toward the house, combing the ground as he went for anything that looked like a place to hide the sacred stone, but by the time he reached the open front lawn of the mansion, the torch light flickering across green blades of grass, he had still come up empty. A breeze blew through the yard and Antonio felt a chill on his skin. Across the lawn, a wide set of steps led up to a veranda outfitted with porch furniture.

He strode across the lawn, setting off pinpoints of light with his feet as he walked —fireflies, he supposed, though they were a rainbow of colors, not only yellow or green. He ascended the steps, boards creaking beneath his feet, and then walked across the veranda to the front door. A stout wooden affair with an ornate brass fixture consisting of a knocker made to resemble a stylized planet Earth, Antonio raised his hand to grip it but then reconsidered. The knock would be loud in the serene stillness. Maybe the door would be open?

He reached out and gripped the handle, but no, it was locked. And then he noticed an electronic keypad set into the door frame. He hadn't seen it when he walked up, but he supposed it was because he'd been focused on the door handle. He studied the LED display and saw eight asterisks, indicating an entry code of as many digits. His initial reaction was one of hopelessness—*eight digits, that's impossible to guess*—but then he took a deep breath and thought about what was tying this together, what had brought him here. He reached out to the key pad and entered: 02281972. His birthday.

A soft tone sounded, and when Antonio tried the door handle again, the door pushed open. He wondered how Stel would ever be able to get in here, but then realized that he would likely have a different combination, one that was suited to his particular set of experiences.

Gently pushing the door open, Antonio walked into the house.

CHAPTER 37

A grand entrance hall. Antonio craned his neck to look up at the ceiling, three stories above his head. A spiral staircase flowed past a hanging crystal chandelier and a stained glass window halfway up the stairs let in the day's fading light. The hardwood floor was partially covered with a sprawling oriental rug. Rooms lay off to his left and right, with the stairwell in front of him leading up.

He stood, taking it all in, listening. The house was quiet. No music, television, no voices, no footsteps. The furniture, the artwork, it was all high quality but old, giving the place a vintage feel. Antonio opted to move to the right. He walked to the edge of the room and saw that it was down two steps from the entrance hall. He stepped into the sunken living room and took it all in. Walls lined with big game taxidermy—jaguar heads, elephants, boar, even ocean game fish such as marlin and sailfish.

A coffee table and leather couch occupied the floor space in front of him. A few books were sprawled on the table, and he went to one to look at the title: *View to the Amazon rain Forest*. The cover featured a photograph taken from just beneath the tree canopy, and looking down straight to the forest floor. Antonio looked closer but could see no author listed on the cover, only the title.

He left the coffee table and moved to the center of the room, where he saw an open doorway leading to an adjacent room. He went there, and saw that he had to step up to get into it. The room was dimly lit, but enough to see that it was a strange place indeed. Or different, at least, Antonio thought as he stepped inside. A suit of armor greeted him from the corner to his right, while a standing gorilla was mounted to his left. But it was the walls that commanded his attention. Both of them were lined with gun racks and weapon cabinets.

Walking deeper into the room, he saw that the cabinets on the left held various bladed weapons—knives, both fixed blade and folding, throwing stars, daggers, machetes, kukris, broad swords, two-handed swords, fencing swords, lances, spears, clubs and more... And not all vintage, either, Antonio thought. Some were very old indeed, but others were obviously modern. Someone here is very into weapons, Antonio thought, turning around to look at the opposite wall.

Guns, lots of them. Also a mix of types—handguns and long guns, vintage and modern. Cabinets to the left and right of the guns held ammunition and accessories—clips, holsters, bullets, scopes...Antonio looked back to the guns, to the section where several automatic weapons were shelved, including AK-47s, AK-74s and more. Weird, he thought, but he didn't see the stone in here so he was getting ready to exit back into the living room—this room had no other outlet—when his gaze fell on something that made his breath catch.

One of the rack spaces in the automatic weapon section was empty. An AK-47 was nestled under it, while an AK-9 was above it, and other compact automatic weapons lay above and below those. Clearly, one of them had been taken.

Slowly, Antonio turned around, suddenly more interested in his situational awareness. Someone had taken one of the machine guns, and he had a pretty good idea of who it was.

Stel.

He had to assume it was Stel, and not that one gun happened to be missing from the racks. Antonio grabbed a Beretta M12 for himself. He slid the bolt back, saw that it was already loaded with a clip, and slung the strap around his shoulder. Then he walked by the handguns and selected a Glock 9mm with a shoulder holster and extra clip to go with it and strapped it on. Finally, moving to the knives, he picked a lethal-looking, serrated fixed-blade knife from the rack and attached its sheath to his belt.

Antonio walked back out into the living room, conscious now of his footsteps and keeping them silent. Stel was somewhere in this house. But was he looking for the stone, or laying in wait to eliminate his opponent? The latter course of action would give Stel time to find the stone at his leisure once he had dispatched Antonio. At the same time, it would be tempting to try and find the prize and then abscond with it unseen.

Antonio crossed back into the entrance hall, looked up the stairs, and then proceeded to enter the room that lay in the opposite direction from the living room.

Dining room. Large table with places set for twelve, a bowl of fresh fruit the only food present. Walking along the table, Antonio passed the fruit and eyed a shiny red apple. Unable to resist, he picked it up. It seemed real enough. He took a bite and savored the delicious taste. How long had it been since he'd eaten? Not that long, he reminded himself. He'd had lunch in the internet café, but that seemed so impossibly long ago, like time was suspended in this dream world. He stopped eating the apple because it made a lot of noise, the crunching, he was afraid Stel could hear it if he was near enough. He set it on the table and then, staring at the table and its white lace tablecloth draped over the edge, slowly drew his automatic weapon and backed up. When he was far enough away, he crouched while sweeping his muzzle underneath the table.

Nothing underneath. Breathing a sigh of relief, Antonio turned his attention to the rest of the room. A china hutch occupied one wall, and Antonio examined its contents—fine chinaware, crystal decanters, bowls and the like. But no meteorites. He saw nothing else in the room that offered either a hiding spot for the artifact or a clue as to its whereabouts, so he moved on into the next room.

Kitchen. A sprawling, two-section affair with a granite-topped island and stainless steel built-in appliances. Six rattan barstools were pulled up to the side of the island counter outside the food preparation area. The flooring was very solid, dark wood, probably old growth mahogany or something similar, Antonio thought, The strange mixture of contemporary and vintage did not escape Antonio, but if it meant something it escaped him.

There were many cabinets both high and low in here. But as Antonio looked around, he noticed that a couple of the cabinet doors were ajar, as though opened and left in a hurry without bothering to close them again. A deep drawer was open, too, its contents—long-handled utensils such as ladles and whisks--disheveled and protruding from the drawer.

Stel had been here already. Antonio's time was better spent elsewhere, and so he focused on where to look next. A back door out of the kitchen led to another area, so he went to it and cautiously peered inside. A laundry room, both washer and dryer doors already opened. He was late to the party here, too. Frowning, Antonio retreated into the kitchen and walked back into the entrance hall.

He stood and looked up the stairway. Time to see what was on the second floor. A chill coursed down his spine; if Stel was still in this house, he was almost surely up there.

He placed his foot onto the first step and grimaced as he heard it creak faintly. He swung his new best friend—his Beretta submachine gun-- up to the ready position as he ascended the stairs. Due to their circular structure, he was shielded from view all the way to the second floor, which was actually at a third story height because of the high ceiling. Still, he progressed slowly, stealth at the forefront of his mind.

At the top of the staircase he froze. A creak of floorboards echoed somewhere from the new floor. A hallway ran right and left with no actual room directly at the top of the stairs. Samba music played softly from somewhere up here, a casual-sounding mood that belied the true nature of Antonio's purpose here.

He stepped into the hall and an explosion of gunfire shattered the calm. Showers of plaster dust rained down on him as he dashed right, opposite from where the shots had come from. He knew he was very lucky he hadn't been hit, and he zigged and zagged down the hall to make himself a more erratic target. When he reached the opening to one of the bedrooms, he dove headlong into it and quickly rolled onto the floor out of the doorway.

He scrambled under the king-sized bed as Stel's rapid footfalls echoed down the hall. Antonio's machine gun was still slung around his back and he was still having trouble swinging it around as Stel entered the bedroom. He smiled when he saw the blood that had congealed in one of Stel's socks. Apparently he'd run into some trouble in this strange wonderland, too. But Antonio still couldn't access his main weapon, and doing so now would make too much noise. Knowing he would have to settle for the pistol, he reached under his chest and removed the Glock from its holster.

Stel's ankles and shoes—black loafers, oddly enough—passed from left to right in front of Antonio's floor-level eyes. He didn't want to risk a shot until he could do real damage, because with that automatic weapon, Stel would be able to blast right through the bed, he wouldn't even need to aim. Antonio lay still enough to be a corpse in a tomb as he watched Stel's feet retreat into the adjoining bathroom. Heard him sliding back a shower curtain…

Go!

Antonio rolled out from under the bed, hoping he could avoid a gunfight. He didn't know if the bathroom connected to an adjoining bedroom or not, but he knew he had to get out of here before Stel came back into the bedroom. He couldn't help but feel a pang of regret at not being able to look for the stone more thoroughly in this room, but one thing was apparent: it wasn't under the bed.

Antonio slinked out of the room into the hall and looked down the stairs. Due to their circular nature, he would be quickly out of sight before he got very far down. He cast a quick glance along the hallway, where another bedroom door was closed. He didn't worry about not seeing the stone up here. Stel had beat him to it, anyway; if it was up here, he would have gotten it already instead of hunting him down like an animal.

But something on the wall caught his eye. A framed picture of some sort, only it didn't look like artwork. A diagram was Antonio's best guess.

Then he heard Stel's voice, yelling from somewhere back in the rooms: "The stone is mine, Dr. Medina! Go home and leave it alone. I won't hesitate to do what I have to do!"

Antonio heard drawers and cupboards opening and slamming. Rather than answer, the ecologist silently padded down the carpeted hallway to the framed picture. It was one of those floorplan diagrams commonly seen in public buildings, to highlight emergency escape routes. This one was complete with a You Are Here green dot. Maybe this place used to be a hotel, Antonio thought, and then he reminded himself that nothing here was what it seemed, and that everything here was by design exactly what he was supposed to see.

Consulting the diagram, he could easily discern the two main floors and even part of the grounds surrounding the house. *But wait...*Part of the plan featured what looked like a floor he hadn't noticed before. *Now, how could that be?* Antonio started to wonder, but then saw the letter "B," written in red, next to the unknown floor. Of course! A *basement.*

He heard Stel running and then the bedroom door at the end of the hall—the one Antonio hadn't been to yet—flew open. Antonio turned and sprinted for the stairs. "Coward!" Stel hollered as he unleashed the full fury of his machine gun.

This is it, Antonio thought. *I'm dead.* Whatever that means in a place like this. He was about to lose the game, that was for sure. If not his life. The first salvo of rounds stitched across the wall in Antonio's direction. He jumped toward the stairs but, knowing he was too late, he put his arms behind his head in anticipation of being shot. But the impact never came. Instead, Stel cursed his jammed weapon before hurling it at Antonio in frustration. His throwing aim was better than his shooting, because the gun hit Antonio in the kneecap, causing him to bend his leg momentarily. He used the opportunity to pick up the gun.

Then, as Stel started to bull-rush him, Antonio tossed the jammed weapon aside and withdrew his Glock. He didn't think Stel had a backup weapon, since he'd seen no empty pistol racks down in the armory.

"Freeze, Stel! Stop now!" He fired a warning shot into the wall to the anthropologist's right. That did it. Stel halted, putting his arms up. But his menacing grin remained.

"What happens if we die in here, Dr. Medina, do you know?"

"You lose the game, and I get the stone. That's my guess, but of course it's only a guess. Take one more step, though, and you're going to find out for sure."

Stel didn't move. "I've already canvassed this entire house. It's not in here. It must be outside somewhere."

"I'm not asking you where it is, Stel. Just shut up. We're going our separate ways."

"What happens if the game is a draw, Dr. Medina? If neither of us find the stone? You think about that?"

"Then there's no winner, and neither of us get the stone."

"So we're both losers in that scenario, is that it?"

"Based on what you did, Stel, you're a loser in any scenario. Goodbye, and good luck to you. I'm not sure what happens to the loser if they're not killed in this little simulation. Maybe you'll respawn somewhere like in a video game, who knows. But here's what I do know: You're going to stay up here, at the top of the stairs, until you hear me leave by the front door. If I see you before then...." Keeping the pistol pointed at Stel, Antonio brought his own machine gun around on the strap and aimed it at his opponent.

Then he backed up until he reached the stairs. He kicked Stel's gun down, taking satisfaction in watching Stel's grim expression as his only weapon clattered down the steps.

Antonio turned and jogged down the stairway, firing a short burst from the automatic weapon to make sure his point was crystal clear. He stopped about halfway down to see if he could hear Stel following in his footsteps, but all was silent. Antonio made it the rest of the way down the stairs and trotted into the kitchen area.

The floorplan diagram had shown the basement entrance to be in the laundry room. He crossed through the kitchen and into the laundry room. He stopped in his tracks as he saw the elevator door on the far wall, across from the washer and dryer. Strange, he thought--who has an elevator in the laundry room? Then he thought maybe it was a laundry chute or dumbwaiter for transferring clothes from the upper floor, but as he walked up to the panel, it looked no different than an ordinary elevator to him. Even the brand, Otis, was familiar.

Wow, he thought, walking up to the control panel, even stranger, there was no up arrow, only one for down. Antonio brought his machine gun front and center and then pressed the button.

CHAPTER 38

The elevator was empty. It looked like any other elevator he'd ever been in. Antonio stepped inside, saw there were only two buttons: one labelled "H" (*House?*), and one labelled "B." *Basement, here we go.* He pressed the 'B' button, the doors whirred shut and he felt the familiar sensation of travelling downward in an elevator car. He expected to stop one floor down, but the elevator continued down, down, down, for almost a minute, until it came to a stop with a pleasant chime.

The doors opened and Antonio stared out into a bright white hall— floors, walls, ceiling, all painted white with fluorescent tube lights illuminating it all from above. He stepped out into the hallway and immediately the elevator doors closed and the car began its upward journey. To his right, the hall seemed to stretch on forever. To his left, a sign on the wall read, RECEIVING, with an arrow pointing left. He walked in that direction until he came to an alcove that interrupted the hallway wall as it stretched out to infinity.

He was shocked to see glass double-doors with a modern lobby inside, decorated with short cut commercial carpeting and potted ficus trees. Two uniformed guards stood off to the sides of the room. One wore a U.S. Army uniform, although he was clearly a Brazilian tribal man, with facial tattoos and large ear loops. He wore a modern pistol in a holster on his right side, and a bow and arrow quiver slung over one shoulder. The other guard wore a pressed blue uniform with the insignia of the European Union, and Antonio recognized this man as an Andaman islands tribe member. He was armed with an Uzi assault rifle slung over one shoulder, and a pouch full of poison-tipped blowdarts ready at his waist.

A horseshoe-shaped reception desk was situated against the far wall, staffed by a topless tribal woman with sagging breasts, tusk through her nose, talking on the phone while absentmindedly twirling a pen in one hand. Behind her mounted on the wall were two large flat-panel monitors, each appearing to show the same type of computer model that Antonio had seen in Stel's lab, with the dots growing exponentially in number on the left screen, and shrinking rapidly on the right. A series of wall-mounted clocks displayed local time in twelve international cities, including London, Mumbai, and New York.

The guards eyed him but said nothing, so Antonio walked up to the desk. The woman covered the phone receiver with one hand while saying in perfect English, "Good afternoon, sir, how may I help you today?"

At first Antonio was at a loss for what to say, and he began to stammer, "I…Uh—" while the receptionist frowned at him. But then he told himself just to go with it, to simply state his business, as he would in any other type of setting like this. He tried again. "Hi, my name is Dr. Antonio Medina, and I'm here to collect the sacred stone and deliver it to its rightful location."

There. I said it. He immediately felt better after airing the words, like a weight had been lifted from him. The receptionist smiled pleasantly and spoke into an intercom. "Dr. Medina is here for the contents of his safe deposit box."

A male voice came back over the intercom, also in English. "Send him in, please."

The receptionist pressed another button and a wall panel slid open to reveal a short hallway leading to a closed steel door with another armed, tribal guard in front of it. She nodded at him and resumed her phone call, and Antonio walked into the new area.

201

"Your ID, Sir," the guard said, also in English. Antonio fumbled for his wallet, wondering if he still even had it, but it was there in his front right pants pocket. He took from it his driver license and presented it to the guard, who looked at it closely while scrutinizing Antonio's face. "Born February 28?" He shot Antonio a withering stare.

"Actually, it was the 29th, but…"

"But they move it a day either side to save you the hassle. I get it, I'm a leap year baby too!" The guard smiled while cutting him off, before opening a door and extending a hand in that direction. "Right this way, please."

Antonio led the way into the new space, the guard following behind him. "Turn right, please," he said from behind. Antonio did and looked through an open doorway into a small cube-shaped room. In the center of the room, the half-meteorite was positioned on a waist-high pedestal. A matrix of red lasers crisscrossed the enclosed space. Antonio waited before approaching any closer.

"It's okay, they're just for show. I like that Tom Cruise movie. Go ahead, you can walk right through them."

Antonio was still unsure about it, but the guard smiled amicably and so he proceeded to walk to the pedestal. He held his breath as he broke the first of the lasers, but true to the guard's word, nothing happened, at least not that Antonio could tell. He caught movement above and looked up to see a ceiling mounted security camera tracking his movement. He reached the pedestal and stood there eyeballing the sacred stone.

He nodded, confirming to himself that it certainly appeared to be the genuine article, that it looked exactly like the other one that now lay on the table of the Internet India Café in Mumbai. The guard walked up beside him, still smiling, but saying nothing as he eyed Antonio expectantly.

"May I?" Antonio nodded to the artifact.

"By all means!" The guard extended a hand to the stone.

Antonio reached out and grabbed it by two hands. He gently lifted, not sure if the meteorite was attached to the pedestal in some way, but it came away easily. He cradled it against his chest and made eye contact with the tribal guard. "Now what?"

"I will escort you back to the elevator. Come, let us go." The guard turned and made for the exit without waiting to see if Antonio had questions.

"Wait a minute," the ecologist said, striding briskly to keep up with the guard. "I meant, *after* I take the elevator up, *then* what do I do with the sacred stone?"

But the guard was even further ahead of him now, and not answering. By the time Antonio reached the front office, the guard was huddled in conference with the receptionist. Both of them looked up and smiled warmly as Antonio entered. The guard rejoined him, waving toward the main exit.

"The elevator to take you back up to the house is just outside these doors, Dr. Medina."

"But where do I take this once I get up there?" Antonio started walking toward the exit.

"Why, to the Amazon rain forest, of course. To the place where it belongs. It is why you are here, no?"

"Yes, but..." Realizing the futility of this conversation, Antonio bid the man goodbye and went to the elevator. It was already down here, waiting with doors open. Antonio stepped inside and hit the button labelled "H." The doors closed with a ding, and Antonio cradled the meteorite as the car began to rocket upwards.

CHAPTER 39

On the ride up, Antonio began to worry. What if Stel was there waiting for him when the doors opened? If so, and he was just standing there with the stone occupying both hands, he was as good as dead. So he set the meteorite down on the elevator floor so that he could have his machine gun ready when the doors opened.

Tensing as he felt the vertical deceleration and then heard the chime, Antonio stood to the left side of the door, so as to give him a little cover should the doors open to a full-on shootout. But for all his worry, when the doors parted there was no one there. The laundry room was empty save for the washer and dryer. He couldn't see most of the kitchen from this angle, but he would just have to proceed with caution as he moved through the rest of the house, as he had done earlier. He had to be able to move around, so he practiced hefting the stone with only one arm, his left, since he was righthanded, wielding his pistol (smaller and lighter than the full-automatic weapon, better for single-handed firing) in his right.

Satisfied he could do it, while at the same time hoping he would not encounter resistance, Antonio moved cautiously into the kitchen. In the absence of his opponent, his thoughts turned to what he was supposed to do with the stone now that he had it. The tribal guard in the subterranean lair had told him, "Take it to the Amazon rain forest." Antonio took that to mean he had to get back out of the house, where the challenge would be completed and then he could, outside of this game, fly the sacred stone to Brazil.

Crouching low as he moved through the kitchen, Antonio made his way back to the entrance hall, a particularly risky spot because of the overhead stairwell, which provided a high vantage point for Stel to shoot from if he was at least halfway down. The front door was an obvious feature to stake out, as Antonio would have to stop there, turn the knob, or undo the latch, whatever the case may be, while holding the heavy stone. It was risky. So he decided to cross all the way through the entrance hall into the living room to see if he would draw Stel out, without stopping at the door.

Taking a deep breath, he ran as quietly as he could to the living room. Once there he descended the step and turned left, flattening himself against the wall. He tried to keep his breathing as quiet as possible so that he could listen for Stel's footsteps, for doors opening and closing, or any other activity that might give away his opponent's presence. He heard nothing out of the ordinary, though, only the repetitive knocking of an off-kilter ceiling fan, and after a while his gaze began to rove about the living room.

He focused at first on hiding spots for Stel, but before long his peripheral vision caught a glowing object. There, on the coffee table! A glowing outline. At first he thought there was a fire, but after watching it for a couple of more seconds, he knew that wasn't the case. He left his position against the wall and began to walk toward the light. Just before reaching the table he recognized what it was: a book. One of the coffee table books now had a golden glowing outline around it.

And not just any book, either, he saw with a start, but *View to the Amazon rain Forest*. Intrigued, Antonio set the stone down on the table and, after a last awareness check, looking around for Stel, he focused his attention on the book. It was the same one he'd taken a look at before, he was certain of that.

Reaching out slowly, he touched the cover, unsure of what the ramifications might be. But nothing happened; the glow didn't let up, his finger felt no different, so far so good. So he pulled the cover back a little, testing what he could and couldn't do. Once open, the pages were totally normal, as books go—not illuminated or with any other magical qualities about them—and he recognized them from before as being the same, the same high quality color photographs of the Amazon.

Out of the corner of his eye he saw another glow start up, and when he looked he saw that the half-rock had begun to fluoresce again. A faint greenish hue. Like the rain forest from whence it came, Antonio reasoned. He flashed on the other times he'd seen the stone glow that color, and he took it to be a positive sign that he was so far doing the right thing.

He picked up the stone, cradling it to his body with one hand. With his other hand, he began flipping through the pages of the book, the whisper of leafing through heavy paper the only sound in the room. The stone's radiating light increased dramatically as Antonio flipped through the images: the rain forest canopy from above, the mighty Amazon river close up, piranhas, tribal fishermen on crude rafts…and a few pages later, there it was.

A distant view of the unknown tribe's country near the cave system where Antonio found it. The caption accompanying the photo read, "Vast, unspoiled tracts of old growth forest like this one conceal many secrets, biological, ecological, and even spiritual, within their primeval confines."

Antonio let go of the pages, stopping on the double-page spread.

A door crashing open upstairs startled him, and then he heard the pounding of Stel's footfalls as he ran along the second floor hallway, heading for the stairs. Instinctively, Antonio started to reach for his gun, but then stopped himself. The stone glowed intensely, a vivid green that was nearly blinding to look at.

Stel was barreling down the staircase now, the spiral nature of it slowing him down, preventing him from jumping all the way down in great leaps. Still, he would be here in a few seconds, shooting to kill, his morality blinded by the very radiance of the artifact he sought. But as Antonio gazed upon the sacred stone, it had the opposite effect. He knew exactly where it belonged and why it must be there. This artifact, this piece of space-borne technology belonged to all of humanity, for the good of everyone, and not only to one small group to be used for control and domination.

"Where are you, Antonio? It's not up there. We need to work together to find this thing. I'll make you a deal: if I find it first, I'll split it with you, if you find it first, then—"

Antonio set the meteorite onto the open pages of the book. It shimmered and radiated light so bright that he had to shield his eyes. While he couldn't see, he could hear Stel running out into the entrance hall. The stone and book together made noise, too, like static electricity discharging, not particularly loud, but an energetic discharge of audible frequencies.

Stel's voice faded into the background and Antonio peeked at the stone through his fingers. It now looked more like a hologram. He could see right through it to the pages of the book. Only now, the photograph was more like a video; he could see the tops of the trees swaying in a breeze as a flock of black birds passed overhead, from left to right across the pages. The fainter the stone became, the more vivid was the scene of the rain forest. It didn't take long, but Antonio watched until the meteorite seemed to dissolve into the book, to become an everlasting part of it.

And then he felt strangely detached from everything, lightheaded, but at the same time very aware that he had accomplished something, and yet that achievement came with a side-effect of confusion. He felt like he had after he had solved the puzzle in the simulation with his father.

Antonio closed his eyes.

CHAPTER 40

London, England

Stel seemed to awake as if from a dream. He was standing in the private Bilderberg Group laboratory, the men from the Group as well as the scientists and technicians staring at him with attention so undivided it was as if he had just walked on water.

"What in God's name is going on here?" one of the suits asked, backing slowly away from Stel. "What just happened—where did you go?"

But Stel couldn't even begin to explain it. The event—dream, hallucination, out of body experience, teleportation—whatever it was—was so rich, so immersive and lucid that he couldn't find the words. Besides, he wasn't sure where he went, anyway. The group sensed his inability to answer and moved on. One of the Bilderberg executives pointed to the empty tabletop.

"Why did you return but the meteorite did not?" He shot Stel an accusatory glance. The technicians and scientists closed around him in a circle. Stel hung his head while he answered.

"I lost the game. I'm sorry. I did my best."

#

Mumbai, India

"Another coffee, sir?" An attractive female Indian server pointed to Antonio's mostly empty cup with a long, green-painted fingernail. Antonio wondered if this beverage prompt had to do with occupying the table too long without buying anything. He had no idea how long he was gone for in real time.

Slow to respond, like a sloth, Antonio looked up at her and nodded. She gave him a strange stare, but nodded and turned away back into the hustle and bustle of the Internet café. Antonio looked at his table. The Andaman stone! It was still here, resting as it had been behind his backpack. Unglowing, it had assumed its natural dark space rock color. His entire table looked to be exactly as it had been when he'd left...or "left," as the case may be, since he wasn't exactly sure.

Antonio collected his things from the table and put the stone back into the pack. He left a bill on the table sufficient to pay for his coffees with a decent tip. The he stood, shouldered his backpack, and walked out of the café.

EPILOGUE

Six months later
Andaman Islands, Indian Ocean

A deep pit inside a cave, with a most unusual rock at the bottom of it, a rock containing a piece of technology that came from space. Tribal warriors guarded the entrance to the cave, never leaving it unattended. It was their rock, as it had been for millennia, and they would guard it for longer than their concept of time allowed them to comprehend. Though their ranks had been decimated months before, enough of them survived, having been outside of the village when the slaughter occurred, to begin rebuilding the tribe.

In the village, the reconstruction had already begun. Decimated huts were torn down and built anew, the expanded graveyard was carefully plotted and tended, and new paths and guard lookouts were carved out of the rain forest. On the mud flats, two hunters aimed bows and arrows at a passing helicopter bearing the insignia of the Indian Coast Guard. The chopper flew over their island without slowing, and the men went back to hunting boar in the woods on the edge of the beach.

#

Brazilian Amazon

Deep within the complex labyrinth of crisscrossing tunnels, darkness in the cavern was almost absolute until it opened up into a phosphorescent subterranean labyrinth, within which was a circular cage of stalagmites. The sacred cage had been barren for a time, but now it was complete once again. The half-meteorite occupied its rightful place, the place it had claimed for thousands of years, guarded once again by tribe members who understood not what it was, only that it was important beyond words, that it was somehow at the core of their very existence. As far as they knew, it was as it has always been, and as it always will be.

The sun set over the Amazon rain forest, bathing the canopy in reddish orange hues, and all around the world, another calendar ticked over another day.

#

New York City

Antonio Medina sat in the television studio that looked out on Times Square. The publicity in the wake of the looted jungle artifacts had been greater than he would have predicted, and although he'd received numerous interview requests, the one he was giving now was the first, an exclusive. He hadn't felt ready to talk about his experience before today, he'd needed time to process it all.

He sat on a chair facing his interviewer, a well-known blonde news magazine host who sat cross-legged in a skirt that was perhaps a little too short.

"Dr. Medina, you're an ecologist."

He nodded.

"Tell us, in layperson terms, please, what that means. What is it that you do?"

"At its core, ecology is the study of how organisms relate to each other and their surroundings. Throughout my career as a professor at Texas A & M University, I've specialized in the ecology of rain forests, and the Amazon in particular."

The interviewer smiled. "I think people forget sometimes that Amazon isn't just an online retailer, it was actually named for the world's largest rain forest."

"And river, that's right."

"So your intimate knowledge of the interplay of the species there means that you are very familiar with the jungle, including some of the native tribes who live there, is that correct?"

"That's right. Humans, especially tribal people who live closely off the land, in a way most people would label 'primitive', are part of the interconnectedness of that ecosystem, and so I have studied indigenous tribes as part of my broader ecological work."

"It was your familiarity with these tribes that led Brazil's President Rocha to enlist your services. When he realized that something extraordinary was happening with the people of tribal descent all dying at once, he called you."

"Correct."

The interviewer looked directly into the camera. "Of course we all know the astonishing coincidence associated with those mass die-offs—all of the deceased were found to have been born on a leap day. We already did a special report on that fascinating but tragic event, which will re-air immediately following this broadcast, along with a special update segment on the mysterious secret society accused of backing the attempted theft of the tribal artifacts—it's important to note that they deny all wrongdoing. But back to you, Dr. Medina, or may I call you Antonio?" She smiled at him with lively eyes.

"Go right ahead."

"Antonio, it's amazing to me that, after all that happened, that both tribes continue to exhibit the violence toward outsiders they were known for prior to the artifacts being removed from their safekeeping. They're no longer uncontacted tribes--the world knows about them-- and as you told us, they've seen outside humans with their own eyes. So why do you think it is that they continue to exhibit such predictable violence against outsiders?" On a screen behind her, a video ran of an Andaman Islands tribesman as seen from a helicopter, making threatening gestures with a spear.

Antonio shrugged. "I can think of a dozen reasons, Hailie. But the important question to me is, why should they be any different than the rest of us?"

END

Sign up for Rick Chesler's mailing list (www.rickchesler.com/contact) to be informed of new releases.

If you enjoyed UNCONTACTED you might also enjoy the following novels by Rick Chesler:

Dane Maddock: The Tomb (Kindle Worlds Novella)

A shipwreck off the coast of Italy sends Maddock and Bones on the hunt for a legendary tomb and a long-lost treasure. With dangers all around, a spy in their midst, and an old enemy lurking in the shadows, can they stay alive long enough to unlock the secret of THE TOMB?

THE YETI by Rick Chesler and Jack Douglas

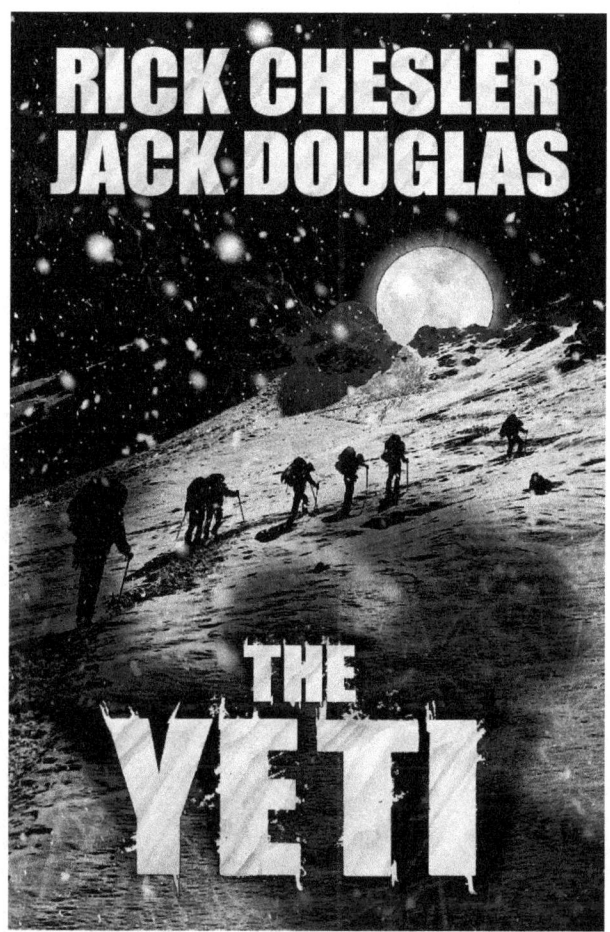

*THE MOST INFAMOUS CRYPTID EVER TO CAPTURE THE
IMAGINATION OF THE PLANET...*

A MAN PUTTING HIS LIFE AT RISK...

*When evolutionary biology professor Dr. Zack Hitchens loses his wife in a senseless
accident, he decides to follow her dreams all the way to the roof of the world-- the peak of
Mount Everest. On the infernal mountain, Zack and his teammates battle sickness,
whiteout conditions, avalanches, the oxygen-starved minds of other climbers - and
something else. Something primitive and consumed with rage. Something seeking revenge...
Something downright abominable.*

Lucifer's Machine (Ogmios Directive) by Steven Savile and Rick Chesler

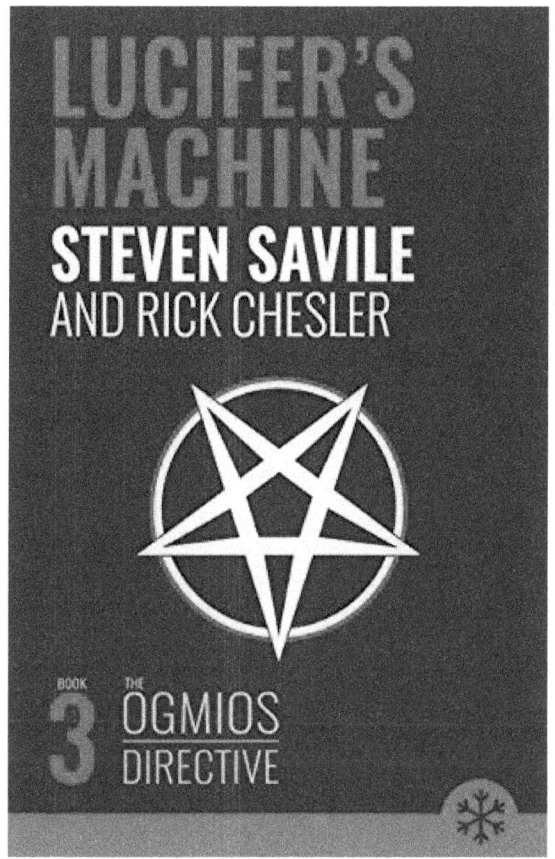

A university archaeology team uncovers an ancient box bearing the image of Baphomet. But before they are able to decipher the box's secrets, the entire team meet a grisly end. All indications are that an extremist group, Al Aler'eyh, are behind the slaughter. A second linked murder in the hallowed halls of Cambridge University tips off Control to the threat.

Enter Sir Charles Wyndham and his Ogmios Team.

Tasked with finding the Lucifer Machine and putting an end to this terror organisation, Noah and Orla find themselves in the adult playground of Dubai, fighting for their lives.

CPSIA information can be obtained
at www.ICGtesting.com
Printed in the USA
BVHW041159240121
598599BV00040B/1099